BETWEEN THE RAIN

Josh Hancock

BETWEEN THE RAIN

Best wishes

Josh Hancock

To order additional copies of this book, contact:
Xlibris Corporation
1-888-7-XLIBRIS
www.Xlibris.com
Orders@Xlibris.com

CONTENTS

CHAPTER ONE 9

CHAPTER TWO 15

CHAPTER THREE 18

CHAPTER FOUR 21

CHAPTER FIVE 29

CHAPTER SIX 31

CHAPTER SEVEN 41

CHAPTER EIGHT 47

CHAPTER NINE 57

CHAPTER TEN 61

CHAPTER ELEVEN 69

CHAPTER TWELVE 75

CHAPTER THIRTEEN 81

CHAPTER FOURTEEN 85

CHAPTER FIFTEEN 95

CHAPTER SIXTEEN 98

CHAPTER SEVENTEEN 102

Dedication

I am indebted to Richard Ferri for his continued support and guidance, to Becky Rodericks for reading and listening, to Tony Acostá for his friendship, to Brett Dalton for his talent and patience, to Dmitry Yudovsky and Stan Sprogis for their creativity and technical expertise, and to my parents for their unconditional love and, above all, their faith in this book.

CHAPTER ONE

Excerpt from *Time Is On Our Side*, the Cherry Glenn High School
Annual, Volume X; (Pam Traver's Senior List of Memories):

"2 Heather B: my angel, we R CA bound . . . 6 per. high! 2
Georgia C. & TM: 2 beautiful for words, luv u 4ever! Led Zep,
Springsteen In Cher Glen? RB, thanx for introducing me to M.
Bolan, U will 4 Ever B my little cosmic dancer . . . Billy Mc:
boxcar races, rides in the Cam, your radio always played the best
songs . . . tell GC how U feel! T-BONE: U QT U, keep n touch! 2
all my friends: lake partys, beer Runs, cruisin . . . is there life on
Mars? ILU all! MOM: if U read this, ILU . . . Daddy: my hero, I'll
B back for you . . . HANK: I'VE NEVE R BEEN SO HAPPY . . .
any 1 else I forgot, it's just the beer light to guide Us now . . .
SENIORS '77!"

The houses in Cherry Glenn were thin as coffins. The water turned green in the dusk and the wind that came down from the mountains stung your face like heartbreak.

This was where you lived before they carried your body away.

Where in some places the lake swallowed the trees. Where the water broke from the land and left bones. When the heavy rains of that last winter came the water rose and washed away what wishes were left to breed on the shore.

A town of drowning trees. There were logs buried in the sand at the lake. It was impossible to imagine a time when the beach might have been clean or pretty.

We lived at the top of the woods in small yellow houses built on top of each other. The houses were wooden with crumbling porches and pink curtains in the windows. The houses had tiny backyards where clotheslines were hung. There was always laundry blowing in the wind and children playing in the backyards with plastic shovels and pails.

Behind our backyards lived the men without families or useful dreams. They lived near the main logging road in humpbacked trailers and trucks propped on cinder blocks. These were called the houses of the dead and you believed it because some kid said he saw a trailer full of human bones. We called the men townies because they were old and had allowed the town to trap them the way places with this much water do.

The houses could barely hold together in a storm. You could imagine a hard rain forcing your family down the slide where the forest trails dropped off to black water. The small beach at the bottom of the woods where the trails dropped off was made with rocks but we still called it a beach.

We lived for photographs of faraway places. The pure white crest of a California wave. The sky turning black above the Carlsbad Caverns. These were the things that made us happy.

The land of Cherry Glenn was inexpensive because the land had been dead a long time. There was fruitpicking and log work and fishing and our fathers tried to make it good. They tried to make a living of it and sometimes we blamed them for casting their dreams from here. Our mothers only looked out the dirty windows of the yellow houses and waited for the dreams to die. The road leading out of Cherry Glenn was littered with hardened fruit rinds and dreams that had not yet inched their way out.

The main road was always wet. The rain had turned some parts of the road to dust. I was a seventeen-year old girl and I had no idea what fresh tar smelled like.

Only the best stories are tuned to the assurances and false promises of life and I want to tell this one the way it happened and not the way I remember it. Memory has a way of changing people and things and not every memory is true of the experience on which it is based. You know this because you are human and humans can make roses out of anything. But to tell a story truly one must be accepting of life as it is and willing to experience beauty and suffering in equal amounts.

So this is not a story of how friends meet.

There are other stories like that and they are good ones. Perhaps this story begins where the last memory of your childhood leaves off or when you heart stops hurting because you have finally learned to be happy. You will take a piece from here or there and there may or may not be a self-revelation when you are through.

Either way the story starts here and it is the truest story I know.

The sky was streaked with orange when Heather and I first arrived at the lake. It had rained hard and the sand was almost as dark as the water.

The light from between the fading clouds was gray with bits of yellow. The rain had washed some of the sand piles away and the logs made for good places to sit. I smoked a cigarette. I was not afraid to die because I did not know how close death was to me or my friends.

Heather and I talked about graduation in the spring and California in the summer. We were going to California in the summer. This was while we were still bleeding and we talked excitedly to keep our minds from the pain.

"In your ear," Heather said. "You've got blood in your ear."

We cleaned each other just like we had always done.

Once the bleeding stopped we talked about the boy who drowned in the lake years before. Heather was superstitious. She had seen the boy walking along the shore of the lake at night. She said he was looking for other children to drown.

"He's the boogeyman," Heather said. "The killer on the road."

And in a way this is a story about ghosts. But we were not ready to face that yet and so we spoke in childish riddles about the dead.

The wind came down from the mountains and made us shiver for home. Christmas was two weeks away and Heather was excited. Her dad was getting her a horse and she said we could go riding when the weather got warm again. We liked to go riding on the trails that led to the main logging road behind our houses.

"A palomino horse!" Heather gushed. "With a long tail and sleepy eyes."

Heather was always a little girl to me. Together we had experienced the awful and beautiful things of the world and she had only grown smaller from the experience. She was small enough to disappear and I loved her for her frailty and for her unwavering faith in our future together.

"Do you think Roy did okay tonight?" she asked.

There was some blood under her nose and blood smears on her chin.

"He puked in the bathroom after school, he was so scared," she said.

We were drinking beer now and watching the stars come out above the mountains. Roy Boxley was one of our best friends. Roy had replaced Hank Powell as starting quarterback of the Cherry Glenn Jaguars. Hank was dead now.

"I've never seen the football field so green," Heather said. She scraped the dried blood out from under her nose. "I can't believe we missed the game, Pam. I can't believe we missed the last game of the year."

Heather started to cry then.

I held her and listened to the lake in the dark. Mist rose from the water and in the darkness the mist looked like tufts of cotton. We finished our beers and tucked our arms inside our jackets and joked around until Heather was smiling again.

"Do you ever miss your mom?" Heather asked then.

I did not answer her at first. I was still listening to the lake in the dark and thinking about how Hank was dead now. I remembered holding his hand in the hallway at school. He was so handsome. I thought about what he whispered to me right before he died and his dying words that told me one day I would understand the meaning of happiness.

Everything was in a state of opening now. The rain had turned the lake shore to mud. Our lives were just ahead of us. They were just around the corner where the main road opened up into an enormous freeway.

"No," I said.

The gray light from between the clouds no longer had bits of yellow in it. There was almost no light at all. The mountains were dark. In the darkness we were as close to the sky as we had ever been.

"We got five years," I said. "That's all we've got."

Heather just sighed because these were only the words to a Bowie song about the end of the world.

"Tell me the story again," Heather said. "About how young and alive we were."

"But we're young now," I said.

I looked down at Heather. Heather was a lightweight. She was almost asleep.

A town of drowning trees. A town where all the curtains in the windows were faded pink. The women used paper flowers to decorate their tables. But in other places of the world children were dropping off just by breathing the wrong air at the wrong time. So maybe this place was not so bad when you really thought about it.

I believed nothing more could be taken from us.

So I pulled Heather close and waited for the rest of our friends to come.

CHAPTER TWO

This was where you lived before they carried your body away.

On weekends the fathers work battered fishing boats named after old loves and loved places. They teach their sons to fish with a kindness that only exists off the land and away from the rest of the world. The kindness in Cherry Glenn is far out on the still water with the rowboats and the mountains in the distance. The kindness comes with the quiet of the watery air when your house is a yellow dot on the map of the world.

The fishing lasts all day. Everything emerges a bloody and joyful mess. The younger boys nap in the sterns. The older boys strip off their shirts and try to impress their fathers with jackknives and cannonballs and all the other dives from childhood.

"Did you see that splash, Dad? Not a drop on board!"

"I'm working out, old man. Let's have a competition, Dad. Ten bucks on the biggest benchpress!"

The fathers are sometimes tired. They wear their fishing shirts open and the furrows in their skin show how old they are. Their skin turns brown in the summer. They reflect on former days in San

Francisco and Atlantic City. They fret over the graduation of their daughters in June.

The sun turns the mountains orange. Then the sun disappears behind the mountains and the water turns calm. The fishing boats dock in the blue darkness of the town and green tarps are stretched across the boats to protect them from the damp. The tarps rattle in the dark with the falling rain. It is this soft song of the night that reminds them of a day when everything was perfect. The fathers drive their tired boys home in rusted green trucks with the radio playing just lightly over the rain.

The women wait still like beautiful monuments on the porches of the yellow houses. They watch their babies through the windows and wait on the porch for their husbands and sons. The smaller children scurry around in the soft glow of the porch lights like puppies.

And then the fathers come up the hills with their buckets of dead fish and their arms around the muscled shoulders of their boys. The sun shines on them through the trees that flank the houses. As years pass the fathers move slower and after many years the boys are the ones carrying the buckets of dead fish up the hills in the dying sun. The fathers accept this change because they see mortality as the great equalizer of life and no man is exempt from death the way some people believe.

Maybe your father teaches you how to drive. Maybe he places his hand over yours on the gear shift and shows you how to properly grip the wheel. He lets you drive home in the dark.

After supper the mothers will take the younger girls to the miniature golf course or the pinball arcades with the little booths where you can have your picture taken. The mothers glance nervously at the grand prix across the way where their sons race go-carts around a track. The mothers convince themselves that this aching for manhood is bigger and stronger than any crash or explosion.

The mothers gather in the concession area where there are picnic tables and umbrellas and comfortable places to sit. Sometimes they sit and talk and sometimes they stand quietly at the edge of the golf course and watch the stars fall through the pines of Cherry Glenn.

When the mothers are in the mood for talking they discuss vacations they may or may not take and aspirations they do not always share with their husbands. The mothers fret over the graduation of their sons in June.

The mothers work in the pharmacies and the used clothing stores and the shops filled with machines and fabrics. They work as shift supervisors at the big grocery near the freeway outside of town. They encourage their daughters to strive for more than this. But then they cry when their daughters leave in pursuit of their dreams.

Maybe your mother gets out before you do. Maybe before she leaves you share a painful moment that shapes the rest of your adolescence.

The daughters are silently considered the biggest dreamers of the bunch. They hear the roar of the freeway in their sleep.

The daughters dance slowly at the winter formals and they kiss slowly and they weep with barely a whisper. They take sips of liquor beneath floating pink streamers in the gym and in these drunken visions see accomplished and wondrous things. The daughters often excel in school. They are aware that every solitary life moment has blossoming abilities.

The girls here pity isolation and secretly fear independence. The girls long to feel male forms to test their love and confirm their loveliness. They tire of keeping their hair in neat bundles. They hear the wind in your hair is magical. They hear leaning over the lap of a boy to check an impossible speedometer is the white edge of heaven.

And you become a bit lonesome when you think about how young you used to be. You resign yourself to your childhood because that was when the people you loved most were alive and happy and exploding with love for you.

The docks are quiet at night. The boats knock each other gently in the dark.

My hometown relishes its own violent silence.

CHAPTER THREE

The sun always seems to rise early when you are a child in school and the frost on the flowers would melt and the grass looked wet in the morning. In the morning flowers from the trees blew across the baseball diamond and stuck to the wet slides and swings. At recess we scraped sap from the locust trees to see and feel the mystery of it all on our fingertips. These are some of the memories you might have from when you were growing up and you remember them differently each time because pleasant childhood memories are like that.

But the truth of this story is that this is also where your dreams were destroyed and this is more difficult to remember. If you were not careful you would look behind the school and see the barren field and the dried stalks of brush and the houses no one lived in anymore. You might remember feeling your life was just as empty and it was frightening to think you would have to stay young a long time. You might remember wanting to grow older so that you could forget the pains of your youth.

I cannot remember how my group of friends came together. Or maybe I do remember but I have decided not to tell that story. This is not a story of how friends meet or how they came to love each other. It is only a story of that horrible last night at the lake when I realized that what you read in books about death really was true. Your life really does flash before your eyes right before you die.

Billy McKenna hung oil lamps from the trees and the water was swirling and dark where the land dropped off and the shallows began. Tony tossed his beers around and the beer cans had ice in the rims.

This was right before the world ended and this was what I saw right before I died.

I saw Danielle and Heather smashing a tetherball so hard the skin on their knuckles broke. Georgia Cates was teaching us new hopscotch songs and we knotted our shoelaces a secret way so we would never trip. I saw us dancing in the Christmas pageant. The girls dressed as elves and the boys dressed as reindeer. The reindeer led a procession of elves and holiday fairies for the parents.

I saw little Hank Powell and Roy Boxley outfitting sleighs with garlands and candy canes.

Death followed us a little bit the way loneliness does some people. I saw Heather sick and perspiring in her bedroom and Roy Boxley in the hospital after he broke his collarbone in junior football. But we were still children then and we ran very fast and death could not keep up with us through the changing seasons and years.

I saw Billy and Roy racing boxcars down the street. The wind blew their hair back and they were laughing. The street was dangerous because you could not see the cars coming around the bend.

"Faster!" Roy Boxley cried.

"Turn coming up!" Billy shouted.

"Turn, turn, turn!"

I saw Hank standing beside me. He almost never swore or said mean things about the girls in our class. The sun was in his hair and his eyes were blue. I liked him the most.

I saw the laces of my sneaker get snagged in the spokes of my bicycle. Hank carried me back to my house and explained to my father what had happened. I saw Hank icing my foot and showing me

HANC

how to keep it elevated on a pillow. I saw the pair of silver shoelaces he bought me the next day.

I saw Georgia blushing over Billy. I saw the cover of her slam book with his name written all over the pages. Georgia developed a sudden interest in muscle cars and movies with Dennis Hopper.

Billy gave Georgia a plastic model of a GTO for her birthday. He helped her paint the hood and fenders. I saw it sitting in the sunlight on the bureau next to her bed.

In the seventh grade we went to dances at the Cherry Glenn Community Center.

I saw pink streamers floating from the rafters. The chaperones walked the dance floor to keep the kids from kissing or dancing too close. Heather and I had our first dances.

I saw myself dancing with Hank. He touched my hair like he was afraid of how much he might grow to love me.

I saw us as children running along the muddy rim of the beach. I saw us as children falling in the shallows. I saw us as children with beach pails and children with dreams as unbelievable as the moon.

I saw Danielle sliding down the muddy shoots that disappeared into the lake.

Roy and Hank were standing near the jetty where the rowboats were kept. They held fishing poles. Their hair was wet and they were smiling and there were life vests at their feet.

I saw Heather spinning wildly in a cylinder of silver rain.

Tony stood in a skim of white water with the sun dropping behind him.

And before the world ended I saw myself standing where the beach arced wide to the north of the lake. Grass was stuck to my knees because I had crawled through the brush to get there. I was only a child with grass stuck to my knees. Beyond my line of vision I saw the lake turn into a cove so big that a child could dream of its size and never get tired.

CHAPTER FOUR

My mother lived with me for longer than the mothers of my friends. So for this reason I am told to feel half-loved and told that half-love is better because you are not as crushed when it ends.

My mother took me on long scenic drives through Cherry Glenn. I liked watching my mother drive. Her hair fell across her forehead like lace and sometimes the wind through the open window of the car lifted her hair in perfect red sails.

She drove to the bakery first. She bought coffee for herself and orange juice for me. She bought jelly doughnuts and rolls with melted butter. Then we got back into the car and drove to the lake.

The fishing boats were out since the dawn and all the townies were either at work or inside the Last Watch Bar. The wood of the jetty was slippery beneath our feet and we were careful not to fall.

The lake bobbed quietly in the soft afternoon wind that came down from the mountains. The lake was full of secrets and perhaps my mother had taken me there to discover them hidden beneath the blinding sunlight on the water.

We parked on the embankment above the dock and ate our breakfast in the morning sun.

During this time my mother told me stories from her childhood. My grandfather was a locksmith. He taught my mother how to swim using a kickboard and a stopwatch to time her laps. My grandmother taught my mother how to cook and to write checks and to be selfish.

After the sunrise my mother and I collected only the flattest and smoothest rocks along the rim of the beach. We rolled our pant legs up to our knees and kicked our shoes off at the shore. My mother wore plastic shoes and flared blue jeans. Inside the plastic shoes her toes wiggled like fishtails. She was really beautiful. She showed me how to make a necklace out of the small smooth rocks using a pocketknife and a piece of string.

The early afternoons would warm up as the sun lengthened above the water and turned the sky around it white. My mother drove carefully down the narrow main road that curved around the woods. I liked watching the woods rush by the window of the car. We had to drive very slowly because sometimes there were deer at the side of the road.

In the afternoons we hiked through the forest between the logging roads and the houses. The trees were tall here and even in the clearings where the brush spread out it was still quite dark. My mother was a considerate hiker. She held my hand when the landscape was steep. When we reached the main logging road we turned left and cut back down through the forest where there was another trail. The trail led to a creek and at the edge where the land broke to water we watched the minnows darting between the stones.

For lunch we returned to the lake. My mother brought egg sandwiches and apple juice. She tied her red hair up with ribbon so she could eat.

After lunch we washed our hands in the cold green water and I listened as my mother told me about all the times she had fallen in love. She told me about all the times a man had hurt her and I learned the difference between love and desire. I knew at an early age that my experiences as a child would be of a similar dual nature.

"Because a man is one thing or another, Pammy," my mother said. "He cannot be both. He cannot love and hate you. He can only do one or the other."

"Does Daddy love you?" I asked.

"Your daddy hates me," my mother said. "That's why I'm leaving. And I want you to promise me you'll leave too one day. Don't spend the rest of your life here. You'll be dead without even knowing it."

"But I love you. Isn't that enough to make you stay?"

She put her hand in my hair. She always put her hand in my hair before she cried.

"No," she said. She started to cry then and the tears rolled off of her nose.

"Oh, you were so close to dying when you were born. You weighed only two little baby pounds. Two little baby pounds with two little baby hairs on top."

My mother cried and we sat with our legs hanging over the jetty. The water was black beneath us and you could not see anything beneath the surface. I watched my mother cry while the black water glinted in the sunlight and the wind came down stronger from the mountains. The day was ending and the wind was making small ripples on the water.

"And when you didn't die no one could believe it. We washed you in a little green mixing bowl and no one could believe you didn't die. That tells me you're destined for more than this life. Because if you weren't you would've died just then. You'd be as dead as this water, or that falling sun, or the moon that will take its place.

"I am only telling you this because there is no one to take care of you now," my mother said. "So this will teach you. This will teach you how only to care about yourself."

Night arrived impatiently and the sky was turning black fast. The leather seats of the car had cooled. I was exhausted from the long day. The water and conversation and food had made me tired.

I tried falling asleep so I would not have to think about how my life was suddenly changing. In my incomplete dreams I could hear my mother sobbing quietly in the car.

To keep herself from crying my mother sang songs by Tommy James and Barbara Lewis. She sang and she cried and I stopped trying to fall asleep so I could listen to her without interruption.

This dual nature haunted my adolescence. The lake called to me with conflicting words and emotions. The scenic drives through Cherry Glenn with my mother ended when time progressed and innocence became an indeterminable thing.

"Do you ever miss your mom?" Heather asked on that last night at the lake.

I did not answer her at first. I was still listening to the lake in the dark and thinking about how Hank was dead now and what California would be like knowing that he was dead.

At night my mother would go for long drives alone. The headlights of her car would cut past my bedroom window and I knew she was gone for the night. I knew she was chasing dreams that had nothing to do with me or the man she married.

I would slip quietly out of bed and sleep with my father.

Dad usually fell asleep in front of the midnight news. There was never enough room to climb into his arms and so I stretched out near his feet. Sometimes his socks were different colors. Sometimes they had holes in them. His breath while he was sleeping was as soft as the whir of a toy helicopter.

There were buckets and enamel cups placed throughout the house to collect the rain that dripped through the roof. I listened to the rain gather in the buckets and enamel cups and tried to think of a time when things would be happier for me and my family. The rain filled the buckets and cups and I could tell when they were overflowing by the kind of sound the rain made on those circular skims of water.

I was not supposed to catch my mother leaving us. I found her in the kitchen when I woke up to get a Coke.

She had two bags against the front door and when she saw me

she started to cry. Her red hair was limp against her face and she was crying and she still looked beautiful in the somber light of the kitchen.

I waited for her to say, "I love you, Pammy."

I waited for her to say, "Let's go wake up Daddy."

But I was only a child then and these imagined words had yet to become hallucinations. I did not know what else to do but to hold her. She was my mother and I would never really be her daughter again.

I hugged her and smelled her clothes for the last time and the perfume on her wrists. My father was asleep down the hall. I was saying goodbye to my mother in the house where I grew up. I was only nine. The floor of the kitchen was slippery with rain.

My mother scooped me up and sat me down on the counter next to the oven. We had oven mitts in the shape of tropical fish and my mother put one on and nibbled at me with it. We laughed for a little while the way people do when they are anxious or afraid. There was moonlight through the window and frost on the windowpane and I was frightened that adulthood was the result of leaving your loved ones behind.

"Do you need a Kleenex?" I asked.

"No thanks, Frogger," she said. Frogger was a name she sometimes called me. The name was from an old video game we used to play together in the arcades.

I told her she better get her coat then. I knew she was leaving.

"What do you want to be?" my mother asked. "We never talked about those kinds of things and now there's no time."

"I want to be with you," I said.

"But that's nothing to be," my mother said.

"Just don't go," I said. "That's what I want to be. I want to be the person that makes you not go."

My mother held me against her chest. "You didn't see me, Pam," she said.

She kept kissing the top of my head and breathing in the smell of my hair. "You didn't see me," she said again. And then she was gone and had not even taken her bags.

I sat on the cold kitchen counter in a nightgown and socks. There was rain on the floor. I could still feel her kisses in my hair and smell the perfume on her wrists.

My father came into my room the next morning. "She's gone," he said.

I played dumb. I had been up crying the whole night.

"We'll be okay," my father said.

We had open-faced cheeseburgers for lunch that afternoon and my father burned the pan.

His mouth full of burger, my father asked, "Do you think she'll come back?"

My mother had waited for the dreams to die and then she left. There had been dreams of love and dreams of happiness and sometimes even dreams of another baby. But these dreams were dead now and my father and I were left alone in the house.

Once my mother was gone I tried not to remind my father of anything sad. And so I never laughed like her or wore my hair the way she did. I never told stories about her or asked why she left. I became overwhelmed with joy when I did something to make my father smile. I cried when he said I reminded him of my mother.

But sometimes I could not keep my memories of her from him and these are the times I remember most.

I remember listening to the wind outside my bedroom window at night. The wind carried noises in the dark and as a child I used these noises to help me sleep. Sometimes it was the tinkling of wind chimes. Sometimes it was the barking of a dog from far away or soft music from another house. Sometimes it was the sound of laundry flapping on a clothesline and sometimes it was just the wind blowing gently through the willow trees.

But sometimes her voice was carried on the wind. She would speak to me just outside my window but she would never come in. I asked my mother many times to come in and sing me to sleep but she never would. It was just a soft voice I was pretending to hear carried on the wind and even at a young age I knew it was not true. She was never coming back and so I imagined her soft voice carried on the wind in the dark and I always asked that voice to stay longer than it did. When the wind was just the wind again I would start to cry. I knew that I was getting older and that crying should not come so easily. But when the wind became just the wind again I could not help it.

One night my father came in to the sound of my crying. I tried to hide my tears in my pillow because I was embarrassed. My father probably never heard voices on the wind in the dark. He probably knew the wind was always just the wind and that your memories of someone could not be carried there the way you carry something in your arms.

He sat down beside me. He was wearing the pajamas I had once given him for Christmas. There were pictures of footballs on the pajamas and there were small holes in the knees because they were his favorite pair. He put his hand in my hair and we remained there for a long time without saying anything. The wind was just the wind and the dark was just the dark. There were no sounds coming from anywhere and finally I stopped crying.

"Why were you crying?" my father asked.

The wind was blowing gently through the willow trees. I tried hard to be strong and not to cry.

"Because I miss Mom," I said.

My father stopped running his hand through my hair. He stopped looking at me and turned to face the window. The moon was bright on his face. I almost could not look at him. I knew then that he heard her voice on the wind too.

There were tears in his eyes. My father was trying hard to be strong and not to cry.

"I want to show you what I do when I miss your mom," he said. He opened his other hand and held up a wooden rosary. The beads were very small and the cross dangling at the place where the beads met was chipped at the corner. We were not a very religious family and I had never seen the rosary before. But my father held it in his hand for a long time. We looked at the rosary together without saying anything. The sounds of the dark picked up again. I could hear the wind chimes and the dogs put out for the night. But it was just my father and me. There were no human voices on the wind making us feel pain or sadness or fear.

"When I miss her, I can't sleep," my father said. "Does that happen to you, too?"

"Daddy, I can never sleep," I said, and I pushed myself closer to him and rested my head on his knee. His pajamas were very soft and he put his hand in my hair again.

"So I say a prayer on each bead, starting at the top and working my way down to the cross," he said. "And I always think I'll still be awake when I reach the top again. But I never am. I always fall asleep before I even reach the bottom."

I sat up in bed. My father was still holding the rosary in his hand and the moon was still bright on his face.

"Do you pray for Mom to come home?" I asked.

"No," my father said. "I only pray for things I know can actually happen. And your mother is not ever coming home."

The way my father said this did not make me sad. I did not have to try to be so strong anymore. I was already growing stronger as I sat there. I was beginning to realize that this was sometimes the way life worked.

"I pray that I will always remember her," my father said. "I pray that I won't get so old that I won't be able to remember what she looks like."

There was another long moment where my father and I did not speak to each other. He placed the rosary into my hand and everything in the room was quiet. The dogs had gone to sleep. The wind had died down. The only sound was our breathing and it was very soft. We said goodnight and my father left the room.

I slept soundly that night and for many nights after. My father never asked for the rosary back. It was his way of telling me to always keep the prayers for my mother to myself.

CHAPTER FIVE

We felt out of place among the asphalt and the wires and the town. We went down to the lake as often as we could.

We parked our cars behind the Last Watch Bar at the top of the woods and made our way down through the brush. Someone always brought a radio. We loved David Bowie. We understood the concept of the alien.

At the bottom of the woods the earth dropped away and the shallows stretched on to the deeper parts of the lake. We had played in the shallows as children when we were afraid to swim past where our feet could touch. The lake turned into a cove and you could not tell where the cove ended and the sky began. The sky was usually gray just above the water but it turned blue further up where the clouds were. The sky was always changing colors.

At night the townies would get drunk at the Last Watch. Then they drove home in the dark with their rifles thrown in the backseat of their trucks and we were left alone on the lake.

The rain fell in thick ropes in the winter and the rain rattled the canvases of the tents the kids brought down to the lake. The rain gathered in our hair and in our clothes. At night our bedsheets were wet with the rain and you could smell it on your skin the next day at school. The sky fell in silver needles.

The trees surrounding the lake were so tall you could not see where they ended. Where some tall trees used to be there were only severed trunks. The town had come to take these ephemeral pieces from us.

The clouds drooped low to the earth on silver springs. The sky was blue between them. Heather was stoned most of the time. She said the sky was floating with people and white horses and sometimes you felt like you were in two places at once.

From the lake the lights of the town shone like impossible dreams.

You could hardly see the main road from the lake. You could hardly see the trucks or people passing through the town. The shining lights told us there was something more to our lives. Perhaps if we walked close enough the shining lights would get brighter and in the glow we would see the directions in which our lives were supposed to go.

But I do not think any of us wanted to go any further than where we were that winter. We were seniors in high school. Our future was the beer Tony would be bringing in the cooler. Our future was the horror stories about the ghost on the lake.

I fell in love with Hank down there too. It was the summer of my junior year and he had been swimming with Roy Boxley and was walking out of the water when I first saw him that day.

There was so much light in his face. The water shone like glitter on his eyelashes. His neck ran smooth as marble to his shoulders. His torso was tan and his smile appeared fluid.

There was a speck of mud on his forehead. I wiped it off. The exuberance in his eyes was immortal. Hank smelled like a million new summers. Hank was my lover by July and I was in love with him.

I almost killed Roy after the accident. I almost cut his throat without looking back.

CHAPTER SIX

We first made love on my sixteenth birthday. We were in my bedroom. My father and all my friends were throwing a big party for me later that night. My father was out getting an ice cream cake with a football theme. Then he was off to the grocery for birthday candles and hamburger meat. We were going to have a barbecue outside.

Earlier my father and Hank strung party lights through the limbs of the willow trees in our backyard. I watched them split a beer. The heavy and light sounds of their laughter was magical and I felt motherly watching them. Hank was handsome and my father was getting older and could not work as fast as he used to. I liked to watch them work in the yard.

Hank and I had never made love with anyone before. We removed our clothes in the afternoon sunlight streaming through my bedroom window. We were not embarrassed to take off our clothes in front of each other.

Hank lowered his mouth to my right breast. The sunlight floated away. The window was filled with white light and for a moment I could not see anything at all. Then we touched each other with the willow trees shaking outside in the wind and the sun falling from the window. My bedroom was cool with the wind through the window screen.

We laughed a lot. I will never forget laughing with Hank. We crawled under the sheets. The sheets were light pink. We touched the fine points of our bodies. We fell into each other like musical notes.

Our lovemaking was a human melting. The sky through my bedroom window was purple and the bedsheets were crisp and pink and soft. The pain was irrelevant when compared with my bursting heart.

And during our lovemaking we had such muted conversation. When our lovemaking ended we remained very still because our reflexes were still talking inside each other. Our bodies pulled apart tenderly and we did not want to let each other go.

Above my bed there was a row of white plastic horses. My mother had given me most of them. You could make their legs gallop by bending them and their tails were made out of white yarn.

The melting turned solid and we held each other without moving. I was crying because it hurt.

Hank picked up the horse I called Midnight and galloped him across my shoulders and the back of my neck. Hank said that each spot where Midnight galloped would stop hurting. Hank gently galloped Midnight down my stomach and over my thighs and legs. The plastic hooves made me shiver and I cried for a long time.

After a while, Hank stopped.

"I know," he said. "I'm being dumb."

I hugged and kissed him. The wind came through the window screen. I was sixteen. My father would be home soon and soon my birthday party would begin.

As I dressed I watched Hank. Hank balled up the pink bedsheets because there was some blood on them. He placed the sheets on the floor. Hank made the bed with fresh sheets from the hallway closet. He put Midnight back on the shelf with the other horses. Then Hank put on his clothes. I watched him the whole time.

He tucked the sheets under his arm. "I'll put these in the machine before your dad gets home. I'll tell him it's my football jersey," he said.

Then he kissed me. We kept kissing in the hallway just outside my bedroom. We kissed like that for a long time before it was time to get ready for the party.

The sky was the color of salmon. The wind had not come down that strong from the mountains yet and it was still warm outside. The barbecue sent up smoke and the white smoke curled up through the willow trees in the backyard.

Georgia and Billy had gone swimming at the lake. They sat shivering on the lawn in towels and swimming trunks. We all had beers from a cooler my father had packed with ice. Roy and Hank helped my father at the barbecue. Roy wore an apron and Hank wore the oven mitts in the shape of tropical fish. The white smoke of the barbecue looped in and out of the trees.

Heather was stoned. She lost herself in the red and blue party lights roped through the branches. The willow trees moved slightly in the wind. Apples were scattered along the dry grass. Danielle was collecting the apples in the hem of her skirt. Georgia was using a towel to dry off her hair and Billy was putting on his Jaguars sweatshirt because it would be getting cold soon.

Hank called out that the burgers were almost ready. Roy goofed with the lighter fluid. Georgia sat close to Billy and said it was because she was trying to keep warm. We all knew that they were both in love with each other. We drank more beer and Heather got me stoned as we stretched out on the dry grass and looked at the sky. My father asked Hank how many football games the Jaguars were going to win that year. Hank told my father all of them.

"The history of this place happened so long ago," my father said, "that everyone's forgotten about it. They've forgotten the little cases where their fathers kept their hooks and bait. They've forgotten the records their mothers used to play. You boys are going to give us something back. Your job is to create a new history."

My father was drinking the most beer. My presents were stacked on the backyard table. The backyard table had a large yellow umbrella over it. There was a row of upturned soil at the edge of the backyard where the wire fence was. My father was trying to grow tomatoes and other vegetables. A shovel was jammed into the upturned soil like a cross.

The burgers were ready. My father had all the usual condiments displayed on the backyard table. We ate our food on the lawn as the sun went down. Heather ate two burgers and most of the potato chips. Mosquitoes were all over us.

"This is something to remember," my father said. "Because for the rest of your lives no one will ever treat you as well as you treat each other right now."

My father asked Hank and Roy to show him some of the football plays for the new season. Tony got the football from the house and the boys and my father began playing catch in the dry summer grass. The sun just above the horizon was turning pink and the lights roped through the willow trees trembled in the wind.

Hank was calling out a play.

"Play the pass," my father said. "Defend the pass."

No one was taking the game very seriously and everyone was just having fun. Georgia and Danielle and I sat in the lawn chairs and drank beer. We watched the boys and my father throw passes and make tackles. The party lights glittered and trembled among the dry leaves and the boys tackled each other and I had never felt so happy.

Finally the football game stopped because of the dark. My father passed out in one of the lawn chairs and Tony brought the football back into the house. My friends went inside to change into warmer clothes. Heather was asleep in the grass with her face turned up to the sky. Hank walked over to where I was sitting and kissed me on the mouth.

"Do you feel older?" he asked.

"I feel alive," I said. I was kissing him back and laughing. "I feel so alive."

He squeezed into the lawn chair with me and we held each other.

The daytime shadows that the trees and the roof of the house made on the grass disappeared. The night seemed intent on lasting forever.

I thought of my mother. I wondered if she was watching the same sky as me. Or maybe she was watching a sky that was just turning blue and sunny. "My present is that I'm here," my mother said. She was only in my head and it was not so bad. She might have been watching a sky that was ready to rain. "My present is that I've come back," she said. I imagined her squinting against the sky and the sun that was just beginning to show.

My father shifted in his summer dreams. There was a dab of ketchup on his lip.

"Danielle said it only hurts the first time," I told Hank.

Roy and Georgia and Tony were coming out of the house.

Heather woke up and rubbed the sleep out of her eyes. "What if the sky fell?" she asked.

We all cracked up and then I saw Billy and Danielle. They were holding the ice cream cake with the football theme. The cake was lit with sixteen birthday candles. My friends all started to sing. The moon appeared above the skyline like a thumbprint. I was sixteen years old and it was the happiest time of my life.

From Georgia I got a new bathing suit. From Billy I got a purple plastic bong. Danielle gave me a knitted pouch of potpourri. Tony got me a card and a bouquet of flowers. Roy said he forgot his present. He gave me a hug and a kiss on the forehead instead. Hank bought me a book of love poems. The pages were made out of dried leaves and flowers.

Heather handed me a shoebox wrapped in the funnies section of the newspaper. I opened the shoebox. Inside was a toddler-shaped figurine made out of clay. The toddler was painted blue.

The inside of Heather's card read: "To Pam: No one knows the way we do. Don't tell a soul. This is to remind you. I love you. Happy birthday. Heather."

Heather and I hugged. She held onto me for a long time and when we parted she was crying a little bit. The willow trees were turning blue in the moonlight. There was the sweet smell of cherries and the musky scent of bark. I told Heather she did not have to cry anymore because we were better now than we ever were before.

Georgia suggested we all go down to the lake for a swim. She said I could wear my new bathing suit. We grabbed the beer cooler and ran to the cars. Danielle and Hank and I drove with Billy in his Camaro. Georgia sat up front with Billy. Tony and Heather drove with Roy in his truck.

I looked at the town through the window of the car. The lights from the porches were soft in the night. Children were appearing out of nowhere from walls of brush. The town lights appeared in flashes of promise. It was just a very peaceful time.

"This is probably the quietest town in history," Danielle said. There was a David Bowie tape playing on the radio and Hank put his arm around me in the backseat of the car.

"Look at all of its soft spots," Georgia said. "At what hasn't been killed off yet."

A sailboat was rigged to a truck. Kids were walking back to their houses from the beach. A family was having dinner on their front lawn and there were small children running around a playpen. The Camaro made record time. We cut through the woods in our sweatshirts and jeans and stripped in the moonlight shining between the pine trees.

The water was black where the earth dropped off and then it spread out in a sheet of dark blue. I kissed Hank in the water and Billy spun Georgia around so that her body made ripples on the surface of the lake. Danielle cued up the tapedeck. We finished the rest of the beer and smoked the rest of the grass. The night seemed intent on lasting forever. The cove was entirely invisible. There seemed only to be this small circular skim of dark water. All of the matches were wet and no one could light any cigarettes. Our clothes were in piles at the edge of the woods. The sky looked just like the lake. Filled with cobalt blue water. Water from rivers all over the state and we were swimming through history.

Billy said that the next time he came to the lake he would bring oil lamps so that we could see each other better. The boys were throwing imaginary football passes to each other and crashing into the shallows. The girls dunked one another in the deeper parts of the lake and tried to touch the bottom. We were no longer afraid to swim where we could not touch the bottom and it felt good to let go of the things that scared us as children. Georgia draped her hair over her face so that you could not tell her front from her back. Danielle stayed under the water the longest. When she came up she spat water like a fountain and everybody laughed and squirted each other with water from their mouths.

The trees shook leaves into the water. Heather said there were white horses galloping among the stars. In the sky the trees split from each other and looked lonely. The moon was full. It was one of those rare moments in the world where everything around you is beautiful and you wonder why you had not noticed it before.

But then Heather was not in the water. She was standing up in the shallows that touched the bank of the woods. She was holding the clay toddler to her chest and her little legs trembled and her hair was stripped away from her face. Her bathing suit was heavy with water. She was crying.

"Heather, come back in the water," I said.

Everyone had stopped playing in the lake. The shallows made a peaceful sound as the water splashed gently against the bank where Heather was standing. It was very quiet.

I stepped out of the lake.

"Heather, come here, honey," I said.

She did not move. The shallows were gently splashing against the bank. Heather was squeezing the toddler. She was watching the dark and the lonely trees in the sky and she was shaking because she was cold. Tears rolled over her lips and I moved close enough to touch her hand. When I touched her hand she started to cry harder. I held her against me.

"I don't know how to be happy anymore," she whispered, crying.

Our friends were coming out of the lake. Heather was trying to tell me she was sorry. She was trying to tell me she was a bad person. I was holding her and kissing the part in her hair and telling her to just shut up. The boys stepped out of the lake. They looked uncomfortable. My stomach muscles cramped. Heather continued to cry and in the dark we put on our clothes. No one said anything to anybody. On the trail back to the cars everyone was very quiet and Heather and I held hands as we walked. On the drive back home it started to rain.

It rained throughout that night. I remember sitting next to my bedroom window late into the night and taking the white plastic horse I called Midnight into my hands. My father was asleep down the hall and my mother had left us a long time ago. And now I was getting older. I had made love for the first time. I was becoming a woman and I was feeling very happy. Yet at the same time I felt sad because Heather had cried in front of us at the lake. I wondered if I would always carry some sadness around with me. I wanted all of my dreams to be filled with sun and white horses and books made from flowers and leaves. But women could not always dream of white horses. We could not always dream this dream of children because we did not feel like children anymore. But I held tightly to the white horse as I watched the rain. I held tightly to the horse and closed my eyes and imagined if I concentrated hard enough Midnight would appear between the rain and the trees and the houses in front of our yard. It was a childish dream and I was no longer a child. I was not a woman without a family or useless dreams. And so there was no white horse when I opened my eyes. There was only the light from the house across the road. There was only the rain falling and the white side of the house across the road with the light shining down on the house. The Petersens lived there and it was very real to me. But every night I waited for the white horse to come. I did not know why I did it because I was a woman now. I knew that such dreams were the dreams of a child and I was no longer a child. But every night I waited for him. I waited for the part of me that never wanted to grow up.

JOSH   HANCOCK

We spent the rest of that summer at the lake. I got high more than usual. Roy and Hank spent the summer talking about football dreams. Heather and I stretched out on towels where the beach was soft and slept in the sun. We kept the clay toddler between us and no one ever mentioned the night at the lake when Heather cried in front of us.

The sand was always more dirt than sand. You could never build anything from it. We had to clear the water of floating bark before we could swim. It was hotter than usual and this irritated everyone. We got into fights with the townies who tried to come down to the lake after they had been drinking at the bar. They showed us their rifles and threw beer bottles. They told Hank he was the worst quarterback Cherry Glenn had ever seen. My friends only laughed at the townies because they were just sad old men with nothing in their lives to look forward to. Even when the sun went down it was still hot outside and we spent a lot of time sitting in the shallows to cool ourselves.

The lights from the town above the woods appeared brighter during those summer nights. At first I thought there might have been a carnival coming to town or that there were more trucks on the logging road. But there was nothing except the bright lights and the heat that remained from the sun. Charred scraps of fireworks floated on the yellow air and the temperature was so hot drivers passed out at the wheel. Cars on their way out of Cherry Glenn fishtailed and ended up backwards in the scrubs. Yellow tow-trucks were routinely dispatched. No one ever said that these drivers might have also been drunk after leaving the Last Watch. Everyone just attributed these accidents to the heat.

When Hank and I made love that summer we kept towels soaked in cold water near the bed to keep ourselves cool. We made making love in the summer in the daytime a very special thing. There was always cold beer to drink. We were often hungry after making love in the daytime and sometimes we made each other breakfast. That summer my father started giving me money to buy groceries while he was at work. Hank and I learned the difference between making love with cold glasses of water by the bed and making love without much consideration for each other at all. I preferred making love when we showed each other how much we cared. Hank agreed and so we made love this way whenever we could.

I was going to be a senior in high school. Heather and I talked about buying a van after graduation. We bought our first map of California. We discovered how a library could be cool. In our dreams we walked along the beaches of Malibu. The sun was always very bright in our dreams and you could walk to where the water looked like a painting. We slept in cheap motels and wandered through board-walks with rollercoasters and bandstands. There was always a band playing and the sun was always setting and kids were running up the beach from the ocean. Heather said she wanted to hear the ocean in her sleep. We were going to make necklaces out of seashells.

I never thought to ask Hank to come with us. I just always expected him to be there.

CHAPTER SEVEN

From *Time Is On Our Side*, (Hank Powell's Senior List of Memories):

"Football, 9-12 Capt . . . Baseball, 9-12 Co-capt . . . Varsity Club, 11-12 . . . Mom & Dad ILU . . . 2 all my friends: TM, B MAC, T-BONE, GC, HB, ILU!! . . . Boxer, stay cool, man . . . 2 Pam: U were always the one, ILU . . . lake partys, Budwzr, Springsteen, swimming, sunburns . . . #s 42, 22, 35, 7, I will miss U guys . . . is there sunshine in S. Barbara? Ground control 2 Major Tom, I'm steppin thru the door!! See U all on the other side!"

   The fall of our senior year was wet and cold. The sky was always gray and the rain was always getting in your eyes when you looked up. Every moment the sky seemed ready to burst. The main quad of our school was under construction and the lawn where the students normally ate lunch was always muddy. Someone said they were installing a new sprinkler system. Two scaffolds shook in the wind at the top of the auditorium. They were building a clock tower but construction had been delayed because of the rain. Kids were always late to their classes.

The football team had hired a new defensive coach and expectations for the season were high. There were pep rallies every Friday where team members read inspiring speeches and shared funny anecdotes from practices and past seasons. There were red and black streamers and red balloons and special routines performed by the cheerleaders. The rain continued through September and by late October a small section of the faculty parking lot had been flooded.

During lunch the cafeteria became crowded and sometimes Heather and I ate near the bike racks where you were allowed to smoke. We smoked whatever was around. You could see the mountains past the bike racks and above them the sun was always hidden behind gray clouds. To avoid the temptation of cutting class and running to the woods Heather and I sometimes snuck into the custodial warehouse. We sat on tubs of blue cleaning fluid and passed a joint around until the sixth period bell.

Heather was heavy into dream interpretation. Talking to a dead relative is a sign of good luck. To dream of dolls is a wish to be young again.

"I dream of intergalactic things," Heather said. "Other planets. Space travel. The universe is like a bunch of hopscotch squares. You skip from one plane to the next."

There were bits of red and black streamers in our hair and streamers stuck to our shoes. We kept passing the joint around and holding in the smoke.

"What happens then?" I asked.

"They give you a new name," Heather said. "A space capsule constructed entirely of taps and wires. The new planets are the ones where you can't keep a secret from anybody."

We were stoned and Heather was laughing and draping the streamers over her eyes.

"I'm blind," she said. "I'm the world's first blind boxer. But I use my sense of smell to target your weak spots. Then I unload a series of furious left-handed punches."

We talked about Ziggy Stardust and Telegram Sam. We finished the joint and smoked cigarettes. We were surrounded by brooms and buckets of dirty water and cans of old paint. Sometimes the custodians came in and pretended not to see us. We were content just being quiet around each other and listening to the strange sounds the old warehouse made.

"It won't be like this, will it, Pam?" Heather asked. "In California, I mean. Our dreams won't be wrecked."

I reached into my bag for another joint.

"No way," I said, but I did not know if I believed in what I said.

We passed the joint around and waited for the bell.

"I've seen his ghost at night," Heather said. "The little boy who drowned in the lake. Have you seen him, Pam?"

"Sometimes," I said. It was hard for me to look at Heather when she talked about the ghost on the lake. It was hard to keep from getting sad when I thought about the way his face might have looked when he went under the water for the last time.

"Billy saw him once too," Heather said. "He told me not to tell anybody. He had gone down to the lake to fish at night and saw the ghost sitting on the jetty."

I knew Billy had not seen the ghost. For my own reasons I knew that no one had seen the ghost of the drowned boy except for me and Heather.

"I read once that ghosts only come back from the dead when they have unsettled business with someone still alive," Heather said. "I wonder who the boy is waiting for down there."

"He's probably angry at his parents for forgetting about him," I said.

"That's not how it happened," Heather said. She looked at me angrily. "His mother had fallen asleep and the boy was supposed to remain inside the house. He broke the rules. He ran out. I thought

HANC

you would have heard this story by now. It's that little house just past the jetty on the north side. The one that looks like a boat."

I listened to her story as I pulled on the joint. There had been other stories similar to this one.

"No one lives there now," Heather said. "The mother died. First she died on the inside and no one came to visit her anymore. Then she died on the outside and an ambulance carried her away."

I did not know how to tell her that something she believed in so much was untrue. I did not know how to get the stories to stop or how to get Heather to forget about the boy who had died.

One day I asked Hank to cut school and come to the lake to make love with me. Hank was worried Coach Knox might find out and not start him that weekend. There was a big game that weekend against Pullman High. I said he would have plenty of time to make it back for practice and Hank agreed.

At the beach the sand was wet and clumpy. We found a place that was private. Stumps were breaking away in the water to join other stumps. We put down several blankets to protect us from the rocks. The sky was gray and white and the trees seemed cut off from where they touched the sky. We hardly had our clothes off in the cold. The rain started to fall and I had to close my eyes as we made love near the still water. Our clothes felt strange against our skin because we had never kept them on before.

The rain was cool and had no taste. I was still thinking about the destruction of dreams. The rain started to fall harder. Someone had left a tarpaulin at the shore and the rain rattled the tarpaulin as it rose up and flapped in the wind. The beach was uncomfortable. Hank was not looking at me. We were both somewhere else and nothing was feeling the way it usually did. Cold water was soaking through the blankets. Hank was not looking at me and something hurt. He was not looking at me and then it was over. The rain continued to fall and the tarpaulin rose and blew out onto the lake.

Hank tried to press his stomach against my back after we had our clothes on right. Leaves fell in desolate spirals from unseen places. We did not talk for a long time and I was confused by what had happened. We had made love in an unloving way and I had not liked it. We had made love in a way that two people would hurt each other. Hank tried to change the mood. He showed me some of the scars he had received from football.

"This one was from a game against Jackson. Four-man blitz and I was on the ground before I even felt the ball in my hands. And this other one. Quarterback sneak the last time we played the Wildcats. I was nailed with a late hit."

The scars reminded me of a solitary moment of violence from my past. My memory was shaping slowly the way the body of a child grows. I thought of the ghost on the lake. I never wanted to make love like that again. I told Hank I was not as good as he thought. I told him that the world was an awful place and there was nothing much to live for except trivial moments of happiness.

Hank held me for a while and then we talked. Hank said the trivial moments of happiness were not trivial at all. He said that what distinguishes these moments from the rest of your life is that it is then when you feel the most loved.

"Maybe I'm just an evil person," I said. "Maybe I have the inability to care about anyone or anything else."

Hank pulled me close and kissed me. He tried to make the act of our bodies touching good again and it did not work. The rain had let up for a moment and the tarpaulin was far out on the lake. The woods were empty.

"You're not evil," Hank said. "You're beautiful."

"Don't say that."

"Why can't I say it?"

"Because no one here knows what beautiful is."

He let go of me. The rain was more gentle now and there were not enough blankets. Our making love had left me cold and I wanted to go home.

"Don't you get it?" I said. "We were not meant to have it. Those

HANC

little windows of happiness are just windows. You can't get through them to the other side. You're only meant to look out them."

"We're young," Hank said. "And the young were meant to be happy."

"We're not that young," I said. "We've already gotten older as we've sat here. And everything we do and everything we say all leads up to the same point."

"People die, Pam," Hank said.

"It's not that they die," I said. "It's that they *are* dying."

I was crying. Hank opened my bag and removed my compact mirror. He opened the mirror and put the small oval glass in front of my face.

"Look," he said. "Look how beautiful you are."

He was not being obnoxious. He was only trying to do what boys do when girls start to cry and I did not hate him for it. I refused to look in the mirror. The woods were growing dark because there was no sun anymore and it was time to leave.

"I love you, Pam," Hank said. "I fucking love you."

Hank put the mirror back in my bag.

"Don't you love me?" he asked.

The rain came down. There was nothing much to say or do.

"It doesn't mean anything to me," I said.

I was still crying when Hank said he was late for practice. We gathered our wet blankets and ran back to the car in the rain.

CHAPTER EIGHT

Another year was ending and I did not want to think about what that meant for me and my friends. I did not want to think about changing as we got older. I knew we were always changing and that sometimes change was good. I just did not want to lose any of my friends. The end of the year always brought out these kinds of worries in me. We always went out together on Halloween and when Heather and I stepped into the cool dusk of the evening the air smelled faintly of sugar. Another year was ending and I did not feel any older. The tender pain I felt when I pressed on my chest might have been death slipping inside me or the fear of a broken heart or it might have been nothing at all.

Tony was throwing a small party just for us. Heather and I walked on one of the paths between the houses. We laughed at the children passing in their costumes through the faint moonlight. The grass was taller as you walked further up the hills between the houses. The sound of children laughing in the night can sometimes have a sinister quality to it and we talked about meaningless things to occupy our minds.

"I was once an angel for Halloween," Heather said. "So I guess I already know what it's like to be dead."

Her face in the moonlight was so beautiful. She was probably the most beautiful girl I had ever seen. Only Heather did not see how beautiful she was and I wanted to kill all the things that made her think she was ugly. It was easy to change the subject with her and so I started talking about meaningless things again. I did not want to talk or think about death anymore. Heather carried the clay toddler in her pocket. We walked the path up the hill in the dark and talked about the ocean and I tried hard not to feel sad. We reached the house and Tony let us inside.

Tony had stocked the refrigerator with beer and eggs. Heather and I got drunk off the cold beer as Hank and Roy slipped eggs into sandwich baggies. Music was playing and we started to dance and I started wondering who had the drugs. The boys were not drinking because of a football game the next night. Heather and I tried to feed beer to the clay toddler. We were blitzed. Roy and Hank and Tony were talking about different pass patterns and did not pay any attention to us. We listened to the music and drank beer until it got very late.

"Look what the toddler brought," Heather said. "It's called California Sunshine."

She slipped me the acid. The acid tab was in the shape of a square.

"The toddler wants to be a boxer when he grows up. Pow! Pow!" she said.

We stood by the window. It was very dark outside. We dropped the acid while the boys argued over the use of the T-formation. It did not take very long.

"Belton doesn't have enough speed."

"And Hooper can't block all by himself."

"But it's our quickest hitting offense."

"We need a brilliant quarterback."

"We already have *that*."

California Sunshine took us on a space trip. It was very dark outside. We could see the blue rim of the planet. The window was filled with all these stars and the universe appeared on my thumb.

My mother was somewhere. Crawling among the rafters. Heather began reciting lines from *Night of the Living Dead*.

"They didn't *move*," she said. "They didn't run. They just *stood* there. Staring at me."

I remembered the movie well. The Cherry Glenn Magic Drive-In on a Saturday night. "There's really no authentic way," I said, "for us to say who or what to look for or guard yourselves against!"

"They're coming to *get you*, Barbara!" Heather chortled.

We continued to drink. Roy bothered Hank about the game last week. A rival team from the next town over crushed the Jaguars by more than three touchdowns.

"The starting formation is garbage," Roy said. "Dodd, now there's a running back. Wallace and Byron and John Reed. You want to talk about players? These guys play their asses off in practice for nothing."

Georgia and Danielle showed up at midnight. Georgia had the flu. She drank two beers and had Danielle drive her back home. Danielle said she would catch up with us later. She did not find out about Hank until much later.

Roy said, "Knox should let me start every once in a while."

Hank said, "If you think you can handle it."

"I've been handling it. But Knox has got us squared off in these little boxes. He says I sat the bench my freshman year. Everyone sits the bench their freshman year."

"It's just a philosophy," Hank said. "You don't have to buy into it."

"I don't have a choice," Roy said.

Hank said he really believed the Jaguars could make it to the district championship that season. The Jaguars had not won a district championship in over a decade.

Billy pulled up in his Camaro just as we were leaving. Roy had his truck. Roy wanted to know who was driving with who. I looked at Hank.

"Let's go, man," Roy said. "Hey, let's go."

"Pam, I'm riding with Roy, okay?"

"I think you should come with me," I said. "I don't feel good. I feel sick."

My mother crept down from the rafters on spindly legs.

"Just follow us," Roy said. "I'll try not to drive too fast."

"Shut up, Roy," I said.

"I'll ride back with you, baby," Hank said. "I promise, alright?"

I gave Roy the finger through the window of the Camaro. Hank was sitting on the back of the truck and I thought he thought the finger was for him. Billy floored the gas and we disappeared into the night like ghosts.

"Pull over," I said. "I have to tell Hank I wasn't giving him the finger."

"They're in front of us, Pam," Billy said. "How are you supposed to tell him?"

Heather was holding the clay toddler. The cars plunged screaming into the town. I did not recognize the streets. I did not recognize the houses. I thought I heard the rowboats bobbing quietly on the lake. I thought I heard the laughter of my parents when they were in love and the slapping of their bare wet feet on the slippery wood of the jetty. They were holding each other on the jetty in the rain and there was a little girl climbing into a rowboat.

My father was taking me fishing. My mother was waving goodbye from the jetty.

"Oh, fuck," I said.

Then my father was holding me. My father was crying because my mother was gone. I remembered this and then I did not remember it. But it was happening there in front of me and my father was crying very hard.

"Shit," I said.

"But that's nothing to be," my mother said.

"But it's what I *am!*" I shouted as loud as I could.

Heather held the clay toddler close to her face. "He doesn't have a thingy, Pam," Heather laughed. "I forgot to make him with a little thingy."

"That thing is sick, you know that, Heather?" Billy said.

"I've killed men stronger than you, Billy McKenna," Heather said.

Roy was slowing down. The moon was full. I tried crawling over the front seat.

"Let me out of here," I said.

"Pam, relax, okay?" Billy said. "Sit back, calm down."

"Billy, I'm scared," I said. "Just stop the car, okay? Stop the car."

"Yeah, stop the car, Billy," Heather said. "We're gonna go a few rounds. I've been working on my uppercut. I've been working on my jabstep."

Roy was stopped in front of us. Hank was throwing eggs at one of the houses. Roy then darted back into the street. Billy blasted a local rock station. It was David Bowie as Ziggy Stardust and all I could think about was how Hank thought I hated him.

"Next one, next one!" Hank shouted over the engines. I tried hurling myself into the passenger seat.

"Cool out, Pam," Billy said.

I caught a glimpse of Hank through the windshield. He had a baseball cap on now. I could not see his eyes. His lips were moving. I could not read his lips and I wondered what he was saying.

"Tell me when we were happy," I begged my father. "Tell me something to make me smile," I said.

"Who's she talking to?" Billy asked.

"Her father, stupid," Heather said.

Roy Boxley cut madman corners. Billy was the Indi-500 champ.

I puked into the front seat.

"Jesus, Pam," Billy said.

Heather mimicked the voice of a drowning boy. "Elp ee, Ah'm drow eeg."

"Shut up!" I screamed.

The town lights blinked and hung back like stars. I swallowed bile. My anus contracted and I suppressed the shits.

We stopped in front of a house with torn curtains in the windows.

There were empty dog kennels in the yard and a swing set turned over on its side.

"Yeah," Billy said. "Cormac. I hate that prick."

Billy removed a baggy of eggs from the glovebox and handed it to me.

"Let's go," he said.

He jumped out. Heather scrambled past me. I got out of the car. I was looking for Hank. Everything was dark and I could not find him anywhere. Billy nailed a truck parked in the drive. There was a shotgun rack in the back of the truck.

"Wake up, Cormac," Billy shouted.

Heather blasted the mailbox and windows above the garage. Roy and Hank were pissing on the lawn and then someone was shouting from inside the house.

"I see you, Boxley! I see you!" someone yelled.

"He's got a shotgun," Roy said. Everyone was laughing. "Cormac's got a goddamn shotgun!"

Everyone ran back to the cars. Hank jumped onto the back of the truck. Billy dragged me to his car. The screen door of the house opened and I saw someone standing there as we drove off.

My father said, "I can't help you." He said, "There's nothing left, Pam. There's nothing good left."

Billy floored it. I was crying.

"I want the lake," I said.

Heather was stroking my hair. "We're going there now, honey," she said.

We drove for several miles. The radio played something soft by Fleetwood Mac. My father was gone now and I was shivering because inside the car it had gotten cold. Billy was smoking a cigarette.

"Christ," he said. He pressed hard on the brakes and the Camaro stopped.

The truck had stopped in front of us. Hank was lying on the ground. His legs were overlapped on the pavement. They looked like bloody shoelaces. There was blood underneath his head. You could see it in the headlights of the cars.

Roy Boxley was moaning. He was already out of the truck. "Someone was out here," he said. "A little kid or something. I saw someone out here."

We all got out of the car.

"Why else would I have turned?" Roy said.

Lights came on in one of the houses across the street. There was a little wire gate that led to the house. The gate was open and the wind was rattling it against the fence.

I knelt down by Hank. There was a strange look on his face. He had blood in his teeth. He tried to talk but there was something caught in his throat. When he coughed I saw that it was blood. I reached into his mouth and began clearing out the blood. Then I took his head into my arms and cradled him in the bright lights from the two cars.

"It wasn't meant for you, Hank," I said. "Honestly, it wasn't meant for you."

His coughed again and his mouth filled with blood. I opened his mouth for him and tried clearing out the blood again with my hands. It was hard to do because I was crying and Hank would not stay still.

"Couldn't you see him?" Roy was shouting. "On the road. Some kid in a costume. A Superman costume."

Billy sat in the road. He was crying. "Shut up, Roy," he said.

Heather was hugging herself and watching me and Hank in the bright lights from the two cars. We listened as the sirens got closer. I told Hank it was okay to die. I told Hank we were long dead already.

The cops shone their flashlights and found Hank and I kissing. The cops recognized Hank. The cops pulled us apart through u-shaped ropes of blood.

In his truck outside the hospital Roy Boxley was smoking. Hank was inside the hospital. His parents were inside the hospital. Hank had lost a lot of blood from where he hit his head and his parents called us murderers right then.

A nurse had knocked Heather out with some downers. Heather was asleep in a room filled with military-style cots inside the hospital.

Billy had called Georgia Cates. They were in a waiting room on the first floor. The police were questioning Billy about the accident.

Roy had asked me to come outside with him. We sat in his truck with the heater on and I cried because I knew Hank was dying. There was nothing I could do about it. Roy smoked a cigarette and fiddled with the buttons on his varsity jacket.

"Some kid was on the road," he said. "That's why I swerved."

"Whose house was that, Roy?" I asked. "Who's Cormac?"

"More than one," Roy said. "I saw them. Children were coming out of the bushes."

"Whose house was that?" I asked again.

"What does it matter now?" Roy said. He did not look at me as we talked. He started smoking another cigarette. A police cruiser stopped in the emergency zone at the front of the hospital. Two police officers got out of the cruiser and walked inside the building. One of the cops was a woman. She did not look much older than me.

There was a peeling knife in a bucket of loose change behind the gear shift. Roy and Hank used the peeling knife for salami sandwiches after football practice. Roy was smoking and staring out the window. There were not many stars. I reached into the change bucket and picked up the peeling knife. The peeling knife was lightweight and felt like I was holding nothing at all. The heater was on and it was getting warmer inside the truck.

Roy was crying.

"I should have let him ride with you," he said. "If he had ridden with you then he would still be alive." Roy was shaking. Ash sprinkled across the upholstery of the truck. "If he dies, I mean," Roy said. He closed his eyes. He started to cry harder.

I brought the peeling knife to his throat.

A cop knocked on the passenger window. I rolled it down.

The cop looked at Roy Boxley. "Put out your cigarette and come inside," the cop said.

Roy got out of the truck. I dropped the peeling knife into the change bucket.

"And by the way," the cop said. "He's asking for you."

I ran inside the hospital to be with Hank.

The cop had been telling the truth. Hank had been asking for me. His parents were on the telephone down the hall. The doctor looked the other way. The doctor said, "Two minutes," and left.

A pitcher of water stood on the bedside table. I poured water into a small paper cup and tried to make Hank drink it. He would not drink the water. His eyes were looking past me. I started to cry.

Hank said, "R ad e?"

I leaned in closer.

Hank said, "R mad ee?"

I swept the hair back from his forehead. His eyes were still looking at the wall behind me. His forehead was hot and he was sweating. I wiped the sweat away from his temples.

"No, honey," I said. "I'm not mad at you."

Roy and Georgia and Billy came in. Billy carried Heather in his arms. She was still asleep. One of the nurses came in and saw us. The nurse ran to get somebody.

"Jesus, don't die," Roy said.

Hank whispered something. Nobody could hear him. His eyes were staring at the wall behind us. There was nothing on the wall except a painting of some flowers. I held his hand and brushed his hair back and kissed his face.

"What did you say?" Roy shouted. "What did you say?"

Hank whispered something again. I was the only one who heard him. He was looking at the painting of the flowers on the wall behind us. You could tell he was dying. I let go of his hand because I did not want to hurt him by squeezing it too hard.

The Powells came into the room. The doctor came in next and started shouting at us.

"Get out," the doctor said. "Please get out!"

Heather woke up. She rubbed the sleep out of her eyes. She looked at Hank lying there in the hospital bed. He was not looking at the painting of the flowers anymore.

"Hank, did you and Pam do it?" Heather asked with a sleepy smile.

And then Hank was dead.

CHAPTER NINE

Roy Boxley had a clean record. There was nothing much anyone could say or do. Roy had swerved because a child ran out into the road. Hank was sitting on the back of the truck and fell off. He hit his head on the pavement and died. We all got off with warnings. We were back in school within a week. Roy Boxley increased his benchpressing by fifteen pounds.

During the funeral I did what anyone else would have done. I imagined that Hank and I were somewhere else. I loved him so much. I pieced together the dreams of a thousand lonely girls. The priest told us to close our eyes and imagine an empty room. He said there was a window in the corner of the room. The priest asked us to stand by the window and look outside.

I looked out the window. Hank and I were in a hotel room in California. It was raining outside and our room was just above the ocean. We could see the dark water through the window and the rain falling past and we could hear the waves crashing onto the beach. There were streaks of water on the window in the hotel room. There were palm trees outside. It was our window. It was the room we would always rent and it was the window we would always look out together. There were hills somewhere behind the palm trees and the canyons were flooding with rain.

We turned down the sheets. Every part of our bodies cooled in the dark and we pressed together quickly to get hot again. There were big pillows at the top of the bed. We listened to the ocean. Hank rested my head on one of the pillows. The waves were high. They were crashing right outside our window and the sound was very peaceful.

The priest told us there was a single door in the room. He said that the door was opening now and that Hank was walking in to join you by the window. He said that Hank looked very happy. He did not look like he was in pain.

And while I grieved for love the world continued to change.

The Jaguars football team surprised everyone. They won their five final games and made it to the district championship. Roy Boxley broke the record for number of yards passing and began applying for scholarships.

The priest told us to face Hank by the window. The priest said there was no before or after. There was only this space in time. You can say what you never said before. You can let Hank know that you love him.

There was water gathering against the window pane. Hank and I were making love. The window was open. There was no screen on the window and the rain started to blow in from the wind that came up from the ocean. Drops of rain landed in our hair and on our backs. We spun like children in the dark. We made love with our eyes open. The sheets caught in the wind and fell away.

I attended class and checked with the school counselor to make sure I had met all the requirements for graduation. I did not think anything more could be taken from me because of what Hank whispered right before he died. The annual Winter Ball was approaching. I signed up on the decorations committee.

I made sure Heather and I bought unlaced pot. I encouraged her to forget about the past and told her I loved her as often as I could.

We spent a lot of time walking the trails behind the houses. We talked about all the songs that had made us cry. We dreamed of horses. We remembered all the times when we could not stop laughing and the people that saw us who thought we were just weird.

Hank and I had finished making love. We were holding each other now and the rain was coming through the window. The rain cooled us off. The big pillows were on the floor. We were talking to each other the way you do when you are almost asleep. We did not really know what we were saying but we felt very safe. It was a special thing to feel safe after making love and the ocean was settling down just outside the window. Everything was very still and we were breathing in time. We fell asleep just like that.

The night after the funeral I waited until my father fell asleep. Then I drove his car down to the lake to be alone with my thoughts. I was not through imagining these moments with Hank. The yellow divider of the road was barely visible in the dark and the roads had ice on them.

The Last Watch was always closed. There was no one around anywhere. I sat close to the edge of the water right where the land dropped off to shallows. I closed my eyes to dream. Everywhere was a breath of Hank. Everywhere was a memory. I made myself naked before the moon and the stars and the water. The night opened up and I saw Hank in constellations. He watched and instructed me to points of lonely exhilaration.

I cried afterward. On the drive back the quiet town seemed atomic. The town lights seemed ready to blow. The night drives were heavy with self-reflection. There were times when I felt forgiven for the decisions I had made because of what Hank whispered right before he died.

Roy Boxley asked me to the Winter Ball and I said yes. I encouraged Billy to ask Georgia to the dance and to maybe tell her he loved her.

Heather and I confirmed our plans for after graduation. We bought a used van we saw in the newspaper with money from our savings accounts. The van did not cost that much. We kept the van in front of my house and began recording our favorite songs onto cassette tapes. Heather tried to get me to listen to Tom Petty and the Heartbreakers. She said Tom was the greatest living American songwriter in the world.

CHAPTER TEN

The morning of the Winter Ball was cold and the sun was white in the sky above the lake. The clouds were still and looked heavy with rain and there were large red ribbons on the telephone poles downtown. Many of the local businesses had wreaths on their doors. Christmas was two weeks away and the excitement and readiness in the air made me forget about the past and I was just happy for a while.

In the morning Heather and I had our hair and nails done at the salon. The salon smelled clean and fresh and there was wet hair all over the floor. The salon girls listened to a radio and drank Coke in between their shifts. They sat in chairs next to us and asked about our dates. They told us about their proms and how excited they were getting ready for them.

After the salon we had a huge breakfast of eggs and pancakes and coffee at the diner. We had grown to enjoy the taste of coffee in the morning. Heather was afraid she might look fat in her dress but we had the rest of the day to relax and not eat anything. My father picked us up and we drove home through the town in the rain. There were little pockets of water all over the road where rainbows appeared.

It took Heather and I three hours to get ready. Our dresses were powdery blue. We listened to Led Zeppelin and Springsteen while we dressed and did our makeup. Outside the rain fell harder and my father had to put a pail underneath a leak in the roof of our house. Water was dripping from the willow trees outside my window. It was getting dark quickly. Sheets of water fell from the gutters. Our house smelled of garlands and pine needles.

A boy named Nick was taking Heather to the dance. He and Roy arrived to pick us up. My father took pictures. Our corsages were light and matched the colors of our dresses. My father took pictures of the boys pinning the corsages on. They were very nervous. Their hair was a little bit wet from the rain.

The weather on the drive to the dance worsened. Above the woods in the sky lightning flashed and made everyone in the truck jump. When we laughed I thought of Hank and that was painful. But it was the kind of pain with traces of joy in it and I knew that for the time being we were in a safe place. There was no death here. Death was somewhere out there where the thunder was rumbling and the rain was drowning the trees. There was no room for it here with my friends inside the truck. We would not have allowed it in. Roy took my hand. We drove on to the dance.

We had decorated the walls of the gym in cool blues and whites. White streamers hung from the rafters and some of them floated down and got stuck in your hair. Girls who were not afraid of wrinkling their dresses made angels in pillows of fake snow and the boys kissed the girls over snowy hilltops lit by fake chandeliers installed just for the dance. At the concession stand they were selling blue-colored drinks in plastic champagne flutes and Christmas tree cookies and cakes. Everyone started to dance and throughout the gym there were dramatic and forlorn whisperings of love and longing.

We requested songs by our favorite bands and danced. Billy had asked Georgia to the dance and though they did not kiss they held hands and shared quiet laughter. Danielle and Tony were there with their dates. Roy Boxley had been drinking since that afternoon and I was struck with the thought that after the school year ended I would probably never see him again. For this reason I let him hold me tight and touch my hair as we danced. There was little reason for anger anymore and I allowed myself to see Roy Boxley as a tragic figure. When summer came such convictions would not mean much anymore.

"Is it okay we're dancing like this?" Roy asked. The music was soft and slow and the light was blue. There were couples dancing slowly all around us.

"Sure, it's okay," I said.

"I loved him," Roy said. "I never told him about it. But there are a lot of things we never say, right? And that doesn't mean Hank didn't know I loved him. Love works that way. It can be silent."

"I'm sure he knew," I said, and I rested my head on his shoulder.

"I'm sorry, Pam," Roy said. The light was changing color and I had my head on his shoulder. There were fake snowflakes drifting through the air. The light was turning green and Roy and I were barely moving. We were just holding onto each other while couples danced slowly around us. "I'm sorry," he said again. We danced as the light in the gym changed colors. We closed our eyes to keep the snowflakes out.

The student body president gave a speech toward the end of the dance. She wished the Jaguars luck in the district championship game next Saturday. She said she loved her parents and that she was going to miss everybody when she graduated. Even though the kids laughed off her sentiment there was an unexpected resonance of sadness in their voices for the rest of the night.

Elton John remembered when rock was young. Todd Rundgren sang about a thousand true loves. Roy asked me for one more slow dance before we left. There was fake snow on the lapels of his jacket and in his hair. There was so much suffering in his eyes that I almost started to cry. We walked to the center of the gym and started to dance. He asked if I knew anything about religious conversion. He asked me how long you had to study to become a Catholic priest. He said Catholicism might be a link to a further understanding of himself and the nature of consequence. Roy said Catholicism was cool.

The dance ended with the usual embarrassment. A girl got sick on the gym floor and the gym lights went on and we waded through crushed champagne flutes and streamers to get to the doors. Outside the parking lot was jammed with cars. The lights of the cars were very bright and everyone was asking everyone else where the best party was. The cars started to file out of the school parking lot. It was one of the last dances of the year.

I sat up front with Roy. Heather said she was sleepy. She and her date wrapped each other in coats and nestled in the back of the truck. A gentle mist was falling through the sky and the night was clear. Billy pulled up in front of us and we began following him to his house in the hills of Cherry Glenn. There are some drives you will never forget and not because they contained some magnificent or transcendental experience. You remember these drives because of the way you felt with the wind in your hair and your friends next to you and nothing committing you to any time or place but that one. It was one of the last nights where I really felt happy.

Tony and Danielle pulled up next to us and sprayed the truck with shaving cream. I rolled down the passenger window and climbed out far enough so that I could sit on the little ledge of the door. Heather stood up in the back of the truck. We began shouting and laughing and trying to wake up the townspeople who were already asleep. Heather reached out her arms so that I could hold her steady as she stood in the back of the truck. Inside the truck Roy was holding onto my leg with one hand and laughing.

Tony and Danielle slowed down and cut behind the truck. Roy pulled into the oncoming lane and allowed Tony and Danielle to pull up on our right side. The road dipped and curved along the hilltops and the strong wind ruffled my dress and hair. Through the woods I could see the main logging road and the white headlights of the big trucks there.

Tony rolled down his window and aimed the can of shaving cream at me. Danielle was in the backseat of the car with her date. She was crawling over toward the back window.

"Don't you dare!" I shouted at Tony.

Roy sped up and each time the road dipped I felt a delightful sinking in my stomach. Tony was laughing too hard to drive straight and his car kept swerving back and forth. Roy nudged closer so that Tony could get a direct hit.

"Take aim!" Roy shouted. He held tightly onto my leg so I would not fall.

The shaving cream hit Heather and me and we were laughing and trying to keep our balance. The road seemed to stretch on forever. Danielle reached her arm out the window and I grabbed onto it with one hand and still held onto Heather with the other. We drove like this for a while and then Billy slowed down and Tony cut in front of him and sped off into the hills. Roy moved over so that Billy could get parallel with the truck. Georgia climbed out the passenger window of the Camaro and sat on the ledge to face us.

"Tell him you love him!" I screamed.

Billy had his window rolled up and could not hear us. Georgia was drumming her hands on the hood of the Camaro and telling me I was crazy.

"If you don't, we will!" Heather said.

We were all laughing and you could tell how embarrassed Georgia was by the expression on her face. The moon was full and Heather was covered in shaving cream and her blonde hair was one long sail in the wind. The bright headlights from the logging road were fading now and we were reaching the dark part of the hills. The boys clicked on their highbeams.

Billy rolled down his window and pointed at Roy.

"Just like when we were kids," he said. "Except for money this time. Second one to my house forks over five bucks."

"I'll go one better than that," Roy said. I leaned back into the truck and buckled up for the race. "Second one to your house has to drink twice as many beers as the first."

"You'll lose on purpose!" Billy shouted.

Roy Boxley floored the gas and we sped into the dark hills with shaving cream in our hair.

Inside the house Billy set up a bar. We drank quickly and someone started telling old stories. Some of these stories were about Hank. Heather held onto my hand as we listened to the stories and I caught myself laughing when I was sure I wanted to cry.

"He was trying to fit the tunic over his head," Roy was saying. "And Father Baker walked in. Hank said he had waited his whole life to become a priest!"

We laughed the kind of laughter you would want to keep in your back pocket. In safe places we tucked the pleasant parts of the night away for future dreaming. Soon everyone was hugging each other and dancing and missing everyone else though we were all in the same room.

"It's not right," Heather said, "that we should all be apart so soon. Don't you think we should stay together forever? I'm sad that we won't stay together forever."

We hugged Heather and told her we felt the same way. After a while I went outside to look at the stars. The sky was filled with them now because the rain clouds had passed. There were too many stars to count. The houses across the road were dark and the wind was strong. I wanted so much for Hank to put his arms around me in the cold. I imagined us standing there in the dark and trying to keep each other warm.

Heather came outside and we walked around the small backyard. We walked along the small gate that led to other houses further up the hills. This was mostly farmland. There were hardly any trees to bump into. The air smelled of rain and wet soil and the ground was soft underneath our feet. We walked for a long time without saying much. Then Heather started to talk.

"Do you think it killed a part of me?" she asked.

"It always kills a small part," I said. "Those times in life where there's nothing to hold onto, they always kill a small part of you."

"I wanted," Heather said. She was crying. "I wanted to hold onto you."

"It wasn't supposed to go like that. Nothing was supposed to go like that. But we had to let it happen and parts of us are dead for it. Parts of me are dead because Hank died."

"There's no hospital for the parts of me that are missing," Heather said. She was crying harder now and it took her a long time to get her words out. I had my arm around her in the dark. "There's no underground laboratory," she said.

"Let's concentrate on what's left," I said.

"I want to try yoga when we get to California," Heather said.

"We'll try it all," I said.

"Yoga and disco. And Tom Petty. You've got to try Tom Petty, Pam."

"We'll be different people," I said. "We won't be tourists. And after a while we'll tell people we're from California. We'll use the word 'native' in our conversations with them."

Sometime during the night Georgia Cates threw up on her dress and Billy put her on the couch where she fell asleep. Billy put a blanket over Georgia and then went to sleep in his bedroom. Heather passed out on the floor after her date left. Tony and Danielle and their dates left for an early breakfast at the diner. Roy passed out in the middle of a bunch of old football pictures and that was when I took the keys to his truck and drove down to the lake.

The Last Watch windows were decorated in spray snow. The bar was closed and the old trucks the townies left in the lot were empty. There were shotgun shells on the ground. There was an old Ford with two blown tires.

The ground was deep with mud in some places and I could hear the water through the trees. Water has a way of finding all the invisible places of the world. There was water dripping from the trees and water soaking into my shoes. I could have walked the entire way to the shallows with my eyes closed.

I sat on the bank and remembered Hank. I saw him perspiring in the hospital bed. I saw him with blood in his teeth and I heard the words he whispered right before he died. I wept for California that night. And I cried because I did not know if I believed in all the things I had said and done before. I thought California might help me to change. I thought for a moment it was possible to recover from tragedy and to rediscover love and to find new friends in all the shimmering and foreign places of the world. All of this seemed possible because of the words Hank whispered right before he died. I knew the words were intended for me.

And so I started to hope. Intergalactic things. Space travel. Skipping from one planet to the next. I was still drunk when I heard the voice of the dead boy over the rise and pull of the lake.

"Pam," the boy said.

He was hovering over the water. He was just a baby and he was not blue at all like Heather had said. He was bright pink the way babies are when they are just born. The umbilical cord hung there like rope and the baby had a tuft of blond hair and these perfect little ears.

"Do you remember me?" the dead baby asked.

"I'm through remembering," I said. "Nothing happened the way you remember it anyway."

The dead baby said, "It's easier to die than it is to remember the things that cause you pain."

"I'm glad you're dead!" I screamed at the baby. "You deserved to die! You and all the other babies in the world."

The baby just looked at me and smiled. The baby had two perfect teeth.

"Oh, you demon," I said.

I passed out somewhere near the lake. In the morning Roy came down with Billy to get his truck and they took me home. I slept for what seemed like forever and when I woke up it was the morning of the district championship football game.

CHAPTER ELEVEN

The school had spared no expense. We all got caught up in the excitement of it all and I was proud of Roy for leading the team this far. There were always red and black streamers in the hallways at school and the teachers had decorated their classrooms in the school colors. Streamers were always falling from the ceilings. The lockers were decorated with ribbons and posters and someone had intertwined red and black streamers through all of the locks. The streamers broke when you opened your locker and the wind swirled them through the cold air.

In the morning the cheerleaders were lining the halls with red and black confetti. You were always ducking under a banner tacked up in the hallway or picking confetti out of your hair or from your clothes. The teachers used red chalk during their lessons and gave extra points to the kids who wore the school colors. At the entrance to the school cheerleaders were passing out red and black Jaguar buttons. There was a raffle to win a stuffed Jaguar toy and a football signed by the entire Jaguar football team and staff. They were going to announce the winners at halftime.

Many of the players walked around with footballs tucked under their arms and each player wore his jersey with a shirt and tie underneath. The boys did not know how to tie their ties very well. Outside streamers were swirling in the wind that came down from the mountains and there were streamers wrapped around poles and draped over windows and benches.

We had a pep rally at lunch in the gym. The cheerleaders performed two routines set to music. Coach Knox and Roy Boxley gave brief speeches. Then Coach Knox announced the starting roster for the district championship game. Everyone cheered for Roy Boxley the most. After the starting players were announced Coach Knox asked for a minute of silence for Hank Powell. During the silence streamers sailed endlessly from the rafters in the gym. There seemed to be an endless supply of red and black streamers and everywhere you looked they were drifting or hanging or gathering in thick piles on the floor.

After school Heather and I walked down to the football field. The field chalk was fresh and white. Patches of ice glistened on the field and the team managers brought out an old sideline heater to melt the ice. There was little sun.

The electric scoreboard towered above the field. The scoreboard had been repainted. Beneath the scoreboard were advertisements for local shops. The player benches ran along the sidelines. Empty orange water tubs sat stacked inside one another. Two janitors were picking litter from the sidelines and wiping down the benches and removing scattered streamers from the grass.

The band platform stood at the edge of the home bleachers. The band instructor was staple-gunning a Jaguars tarp to the platform. A student carried two trombone cases from the music room to the field. The cheerleading platform was raised three feet from the ground and stood to the left of the band platform. Two unsuited cheerleaders posted a homemade Jaguars banner to the front of the platform. Near the field the cheerleading coach was leading her squad through a number of routines.

The home bleachers ran thirty rows up. A special cheering section for the students was squared off with Jaguar pennants and red and black streamers. The announcing booth was at the top of the bleachers. One of the assistant coaches tested the microphones from inside the booth. He flashed the orange numbers of the scoreboard to make sure the board was working properly.

The Cherry Glenn Jaguars football team came out from the lockerroom and began running sprints. Roy Boxley walked over to where Heather and I stood in the bleachers.

"Everything's happening so fast," he said.

"You'll do great, Roy," I said.

"Work on the lower body," Heather said. "Body blows to the rib cage. Hit below the belt if you have to."

"You weirdo," Roy said. We laughed and stood there for a while just looking at each other and the players running slow sprints around the track. Then Roy said, "I should warm up. Coach is making us sprint a little before we go home for supper."

We all looked out at the field where the team was slowly circling the track. The wind was already strong down on the field and you could tell it was going to be a cold night. I do not know how long we stood there looking at the field and the players running around it. It seemed like a long time before anyone said anything.

"He wouldn't have been scared," Roy finally said.

We stood there and no one said anything. A light drizzle began to fall. There was no sun. Then Roy ran to join his team and Heather and I watched him go. He did not look back over his shoulder or wave to us. Heather and I started walking down the bleachers toward the school parking lot.

"I'm going to catch the bus home," I said as we neared the lot. Her father had let Heather borrow his car for the night.

"Why?" Heather asked.

"I don't know," I said. "I feel like taking my time."

Heather only shrugged. She said she would pick me up in two hours.

The bus moved slowly through the town. I was still too tired to do much of anything. There were not too many people on the bus and I sat near the front.

The shops were closing. The town was decorated in the school colors and there were streamers caught in the sewers and the bushes. Some boys were throwing a football around on the side of the road. The boys were wearing gloves and it was hard for them to catch the football properly.

"What kind of life do you want for yourself?" someone asked.

I kept staring out the window at the boys throwing around the football. I had to crane my neck see them. In the distance the boys were smaller and looked younger than they actually were. I had not even realized at first that the bus driver was talking to me.

I turned to look at her.

"I noticed you looking out the window there," she said. "I was wondering what kind of life you want for yourself."

"One where there is nothing and no one to care about," I said.

The bus pulled out from a stop and kept going. I could not see the boys throwing around the football anymore. The bus was nearly empty now. I swallowed back a sob. For some reason I felt like crying.

Roy Boxley stopped by my house at six. My father let him in. My father had the radio turned to a local station so he could listen to the game.

Roy sat down in a chair by the window in my bedroom. He looked out the window at the darkening sky and the willow trees shaking in the wind. He did not talk for a long time. He did not even smoke a cigarette. Finally he stopped looking out the window in my bedroom and when he turned to me his expression was sad.

"I want to ask you something," he said.

In his eyes you could see he was going to start crying soon. I picked up Midnight from the shelf above my bed just so to have something to do. I did not want Roy to cry. Looking at him I realized that none of us had been truly happy for a long time. I did not think any of us knew how to be happy anymore.

But then Roy started talking about California and his expression changed. Roy Boxley actually smiled. He had heard of little churches and missions where you could pray and eat and sleep. He had read a book about a religious man who walked all over California and was put up at every house or cabin he came to. Outside the cabins and houses were deep blue oceans that had wonderful cold pockets if you swam deep enough. After a long swim in the ocean there was food to eat on the beach and cold water to drink. The sand was always gold and soft and there were hardly any rocks. Roy had read this. He had seen pictures in books.

Roy said he had already started praying. It was difficult at first. Certain images kept interrupting his prayers. He had bought a small crucifix on a chain and his praying went much smoother now. Sometimes he talked to Hank when he prayed. He gripped the crucifix between his fingers and he knew Hank could hear him. He said he felt like Hank could hear him when he held onto the crucifix very tight.

"I killed him, Pam," he said. He did not look at me as he spoke. He had turned to face the sky and the trees again. "I didn't mean to kill him, but I did. And I can't stay here. I'm already half crazy like the rest of them. But there's half of me that's still alive. You don't see it too often, but it's there. And I want to preserve that. I need to preserve that. Help me, okay? Help me preserve the half of me that's still alive."

I could hear the radio playing from the next room where my father was listening. The announcer was listing the starting rosters. Outside it had started to rain. Roy stopped looking out the window and stood up. He looked at the horses on the shelf above my bed.

"Are these your horses?" he asked.

I nodded. I was still holding Midnight in my hand just to have something to do.

"Can I come to California with you?" Roy asked.

He did finally cry then and he came to me and I hugged him. My father was listening to the radio in the next room and I was holding

Roy in my arms. It was raining outside. It was the night of the most highly anticipated football game in ten years and after tonight nothing would be the same again. I was not sure what was going to change. I knew that I was already changing as I held onto Roy in my bedroom. I told him yes over and over again. His truck was parked outside and I walked out with him in the rain and watched him drive down the main road to school. I went back inside to get dressed for the game.

CHAPTER TWELVE

From *Time Is On Our Side*, (Roy Boxley's Senior List of Memories):

"Football, 9-12 . . . Baseball, 9-12 Co-Capt . . . Varsity Club, 11-12 . . . Key Club, Budwzr Wkend Club, Lake PRTYS!! 2 Hankie: I always looked up 2 U . . . 2 Jag cheer sqd, wish I had time 2 luv U all . . . 2 HB, GC, & TM: wham bam thank U maam, BOWIE nites at the lake! PT: thanx for puttin up w/ me, be free in CA! 2 #s 44, 50, 21, 22, 7 . . . Knox didn't know what he had . . . 2 all my friends, U NO who U R: I wish we could swim like dolphins could swim . . . 2 the rest of CGHS: oink, oink!! PS. Tony T-Bone: U thought I 4got U!!"

Heather was late because she had gotten into a fight with her father. She said we would probably not find a seat in the cheering section but that she knew someone in the band who might be able to get us close. When I left the house my father was curled up by the radio. The football was tucked under his arm and the radio was close to his ear. The radio was old and did not play very loud.

"Bye, Dad," I said.

My father looked up and said, "Wake me up when you get home."

We started to drive. Heather was already stoned. The clay toddler shook on the dashboard as we drove along the woods with beers between our legs. Empty beer bottles clinked in the backseat of the car. We smoked cigarettes and drank the cold beer as Heather drove past the town toward school.

For a while we talked about the lake party after the big win.

"I want to listen to the Bowie tape from start to finish tonight," Heather said. "Even the songs that don't necessarily follow the story of Ziggy. I like the raging choruses."

As Heather and I drank we fell into one of those laughing fits only understandable to girls on the brink of freedom and change. We did not mind that we seemed to be driving forever. The rain started to fall and Heather clicked on the highbeams.

A truck packed with townies passed us on the left side. Heather shot them the finger.

"Vampires," Heather said.

"Nosferatu," I said. "The undead."

The sun had not gone completely into the water yet. The clay toddler kept toppling over and Heather kept picking him up and putting him back on the dashboard. The windshield wipers did not work very well because the rubber was frayed. It was hard to see the road in front of us.

"We're going to be late," Heather said.

She picked up speed. The road was very narrow and there were cars coming in the other direction. I clicked in my safety belt. The clay toddler slipped off the dash and onto the floor of the car. The streaks of orange on the horizon were fading.

"Heather, slow down," I said.

Heather fumbled near the gear shift for the toddler. Her beer bottle tipped and the beer spilled onto the floor of the car. The car veered across the road just as another car had passed.

"We'll never make it without him," Heather said. "Get him, Pam."

"Slow down and I will," I said.

"Just get him!" Heather shouted.

I leaned forward for the toddler and the safety belt locked. The toddler slid under my seat.

"He's gone, I can't get him," I said.

"Undo your belt," Heather said.

The windows started to steam. The defroster was broken and you could hardly see the road through the windshield.

"Forget him, just slow down."

"I wouldn't expect you to understand," Heather said. "You've never understood a damn thing."

The beer bottles in the backseat clinked against one another. The road plunged ahead.

"Fuck it," Heather said. She unlocked her safety belt.

"What are you doing?" I asked.

Heather let go of the steering wheel. She leaned over and ducked beneath my seat.

The car skidded from the water on the road into the next lane and I felt a rush of weight on the left side of the vehicle. The back of the car hit the embankment. The back windshield exploded and the car stalled in a gulch of rain water at the side of the road. There was a vaguely ear-shaped glob of blood on the window from where my head hit the glass.

Heather sat up. There was blood under her nose and in her hair.

"Found him," she said.

She waved the toddler in front of my face and then I drifted to sleep.

Heather was running her fingers through my hair. The rain on my face felt refreshing and clean. My head was nestled on a bed of brown needles and pine leaves. We had left the car at the side of the road.

Heather had wrapped a t-shirt around her head. The t-shirt had some blood on it. The lake washed over the small rocks that made up the beach and the night was still except for the quiet rain. My head was throbbing and to soothe it Heather ran a cold beer across my forehead. Then we drank to calm ourselves until our noses ached from the cold.

"After tonight," I said, "all of this will stop. I don't want to live like this anymore. And if you do, then go with someone else to California."

Heather got down next to me and moved her waist against mine so that we were both looking up at the sky. The sky was still darkening and stars were forming above the lake. Heather had the clay toddler propped up on her chest.

"Do you think it hurt when he drowned?" she asked.

The lake washed over the rocks that made up the beach. Every so often a leaf or a pine needle would sail down through the darkness. There were no sounds coming from the highway. Everybody was at the game.

"It hurts in your throat," I said. "And in your head. Your eyes try to force their way out of your skull. But you pass out before you actually die. It's only when you're floating there, not moving or doing much of anything, that you die."

I removed a ball of tissue from my ear. I scraped out the dry scabs of blood. The beer tasted good and the bridge of my nose thudded with the cold.

"If we're going to California," I said, "then we'll have to get rid of him."

Heather nestled her head in my neck. Her hair was damp and smelled clean.

"He won't get us if we throw him away?" she asked.

The orange streaks on the horizon were gone now. The wind that came down from the mountains made whistling noises through the trees. I kissed Heather on the forehead. I felt like crying again.

"He won't get us," I said.

Heather sat up.

"Pam," she said. "Do you love me? Don't laugh. I know it's stupid. I just want to know."

Hank was dead. My father wanted me to wake him up when I got home. We were almost finished with high school and we were on our way to California.

"I love you," I said.

Heather looked at me.

"Hold my hand," she said.

I held onto her hand and she closed her eyes. With her other hand she threw the clay toddler into the lake and then there was steam on the surface of the water where he went in.

"I'm not going to miss him," Heather said.

Heather had brought our jackets from the car. We put them on and sat on the bank of the lake and drank our beers.

"I can't wait until Christmas," Heather said. "My dad might be getting me a horse. A palomino horse with a long tail and sleepy eyes."

Water lapped on the bank of the lake and you could not see the rocks of the beach anymore. I remembered some sad things. I heard a whispering but it was only my mind reeling back on dead memories and people.

"I can't believe we missed the game, Pam," Heather said. "We missed the last football game of the year."

"It was the last thing," I said. "It was the very last thing anyone could ever take from us."

Heather started to cry then.

"I love you too," she said.

I held her and listened to the lake in the dark. I had been thinking about the nature of consequence and I knew the world was a forgiving place if only some of the things that made you the most happy were taken from you. We finished our beers and tucked our arms inside our jackets and joked around until Heather was smiling again.

"Do you ever miss your mom?" Heather asked then.

I did not answer her at first. I was still listening to the lake in the dark and thinking about what Hank whispered to me right before he died. He said it more with his eyes than with his voice and I knew I would never forget it.

He said the past only moves further away with each day and the past can never be lived over again. And one day you wake up and the past hurts a little less than it did the day before until eventually you forget what made you so sad. Then you are happy and content with life and you accept the love others have for you with ease.

"No," I said.

"Tell me about when we were young," Heather said. "Tell me about the boxcar races and the dances we went to and the time we got to dress like sailors in the school play."

I looked down at Heather. Heather was a lightweight. She was almost asleep.

"Start with where we were born," she said.

By the time I was done our friends were coming through the woods.

Chapter Thirteen

The light from the oil lamps was pale in the rain and the moonlight. The woods were wet now and the smell of bark and wet leaves left a papery taste in your mouth. Billy and Georgia had left during the fourth quarter of the game. Roy Boxley had thrown for three touchdowns and the Jaguars were ahead by eighteen points with two minutes to go.

I told Georgia and Billy about the car accident. Georgia took Heather into the shallows and cleaned her forehead with water. Billy pulled me aside underneath some pines.

"What happened to you guys?" he asked.

"The roads are wet," I said.

"I don't see how it's going to work, Pam," Billy said. "Out there in California. The two of you on your own."

"We won't be on our own," I said. "We'll have each other."

Billy shook his head. There had been jealousy in his voice. There in the rain I felt guilty for not asking the others to come with us. The rain was light where we were standing. You could barely hear it through the trees as Billy walked away.

We drank quickly because we knew this was our last night on the lake. The lake was beautiful and warm in the spring and the air was rich with pollen and sunshine. But for the same reasons it was beautiful it would be painful too. I did not want to come back in the spring and I felt content with these winter dreams.

Georgia brought chips and cold chicken sandwiches. We ate and drank on the bank of the lake and the rain stopped as we were eating and the sky was filled with dark gray clouds. Heather crept up behind Georgia and dropped a baby frog down the back of her shirt. Georgia chased her and the two girls went crashing into the shallow part of the lake.

Tony and Danielle came through the woods. They had left during the final seconds of the game. Roy Boxley had hit Derek Hoffman on an out pattern for another touchdown. Tony tossed his beers around. The beer cans had ice in the rims. Roy would be here soon. Danielle put Bowie on the tapedeck. Heather and Georgia climbed out of the water and we danced and laughed and splashed each other. Georgia started to dance with Billy. Georgia then blushed and ran to talk with Danielle in a grove of damp trees. Everyone was drinking and the cold beer and the cold food were delicious.

When Heather danced close to me I took her face in my hands. Water was streaming down her face and her smile was full. She had the longest eyelashes I had ever seen. I did not have the words to tell her how sorry I was and how much I loved her. I just kept looking into her eyes and thinking of all that we had experienced. It was a long wait before either one of us spoke.

"We'll take care of each other," I said. "Just like before. We'll take care of each other, okay?"

"You've always understood," Heather said. "I don't know why I said that. You've always understood me."

Heather hugged me tightly. It was behind us now. Everything was behind us now and the future looked very bright. Billy and Tony lit a spliff and the sweet smoke drifted over to us. The night began to lose time. The air was thick with the pale light from the oil lamps and the sweet smoke of the spliff. I cried for Hank a little because I missed him so much. Tony held me and gave me soft kisses on my forehead as I cried.

Then some of the townies came down from the Last Watch.

"Get lost, creeps," Georgia said.

"You kids know the score of the game?" the townies asked. They were drunk and could hardly stand straight. "Electricity's out. We wanna know the score of the game."

Their skin looked pale in the dark and their clothes were torn in some places.

"Leave us the fuck alone!" Heather screamed.

The townies shuffled back to the bar. One of them had a limp.

Heather was still screaming at the townies and everyone was laughing except for me. I ran my hands through her hair to straighten it and kissed her eyelids until she calmed down and told me she wanted another beer.

Suddenly the boys were naked and jumping into the deeper parts of the lake. The girls gathered next to the tapedeck and laughed at the boys and their wonderful nakedness. The night and the water were cold and their bodies showed it. The girls laughed at what their bodies showed and the laughter was pure and free of guilt or insecurity.

Georgia asked, "Pam, did you love Hank?"

"Yes," I said. "I loved him."

Georgia leaned across the circle of girls and hugged me. She whispered so that no one else could hear her over the tapedeck and the splashing. "I love Billy, too," she said.

The wind came down from the mountains as Heather and Georgia rolled a joint and the boys were splashing and playing in the lake. The girls smoked the joint. Then the boys dragged Georgia and Danielle into the water. Their clothes stuck to their skin and just like the boys their bodies showed how cold and alive the lake was. The girls stood on the edge where the earth dropped off to shallows and gave the boys clumsy stripteases.

Heather slid out of her clothes. Her body was soft and small and when she moved into the water she went like liquid. I leaned against one of the trees in the shadows the moon created through the branches and watched these fragile young mysteries unfold. The lake flooded with memories. The black water issued a damaged life history.

The death of loved ones and the death of dreams. We had felt that pain inside us and it was a pain no one else had ever experienced because it was our own. The forgotten houses up in the hills. But these were houses where people had lived. These were houses where little girls had lost their mothers and houses where boys had played football and houses where fathers had cried. The lake rose up in pictures from the past. I saw a ghost story two unhappy girls had made from their loneliness and pain. From the water I saw the little things from childhood you never forget. The powdery sand that always failed you and the kisses you forgot about and suddenly remembered. The names of all the boys you had ever loved and all the girls who had ever tried to be your friend. It hurt to see these things because I was older now and I would forget what had once brought me happiness. It was only the sad things that stayed alive in my memory. It was only the sad things that came to me at night and the sad things that made me turn other people away. But perhaps there had been enough pain and loss for me and my friends. Death had followed us the way loneliness does some people and it had removed things from our bodies that we needed to be happy. But death had not removed everything and we fought against it with determination.

It was a perfect night. I took off my clothes to join my friends in the lake. That was when Roy Boxley came running through the trees. He was still dressed in his football jersey. He stopped at the bank of the lake to catch his breath.

"We kicked their asses!" he said. "One of the scouts asked—"

The bullet hit him in the back of the head and I saw his face go across the water.

CHAPTER FOURTEEN

To remember where you once experienced trauma is a pain unfamiliar to you until now. I had tried to forget what we were capable of. I had tried to forget what we had done and to forget how we felt after it was over. The water was still in the seconds it took to remember everything that had happened. So maybe this story does begin where the last memory of your childhood leaves off. It begins with the part that took you so many years to forget. But the water was always there to remind me.

Heather and I were up by the Last Watch Bar on a Saturday night. There was an away game against Lakeside High and the boys were gone. We were only freshman in high school and the townies were drawn to us because of our innocence and our long hair and the sound of our laughter. The townies were already spiritually dead. They had cast their dreams from here and the world had broken them. Their women had waited for the dreams to die and then left their men to rot.

One of the townies told us he could sneak us in to the back of the Last Watch. We followed him because we had not learned to hate the townies yet and we really only felt sorry for them.

I had never been inside the bar. There were peanut shells on the floor and two pinball machines and a jukebox and a small bandstand. Christmas lights were tacked above the bar. It was the middle of November. There was a small dance floor in front of the bandstand. There were white lights above the dance floor and one pool table in the back.

The townie paid for everything. The beer was served in red plastic cups. Heather chewed up a handful of mushrooms while we were in the bathroom. Heather and the townie danced. The jukebox played songs by Elton John. Heather and the townie tried to dance close. They were clumsy and looked ridiculous. The white lights above the dance floor played on their faces. Heather laughed and put her head on his shoulder. The light dropped through her hair and rolled through her eyes and she looked young and beautiful. The townie kept whispering to her and Heather kept whispering back.

The dancing was over. The townie and Heather returned to the bar. Heather started having a conversation with a popcorn kernel and the jukebox continued to play music. A rock band was setting up their instruments.

"Do you want to dance?" the townie asked me.

"No," I said. I finished my beer. "But I'll take another beer."

"The local brew's accelerated assault on the senses is uncanny," the townie might have said.

"Huh?"

"It'll fuck you up," he said.

The townie waved down the bartender. The bartender poured two beers while looking at the townie.

"How's the school annual looking this year?" the townie asked. "Who will get 'Prettiest Eyes'?"

He paid the bartender. The bartender kept looking at the townie.

"I don't know," I said. "We haven't voted yet."

Heather placed the popcorn kernel in her palm and started to pet it.

"Nothing will hurt you," she said. Then Heather started to laugh. The last beer was warm and came back up mixed with vomit. I swallowed it down. The townie had edged his way between me and Heather at the bar.

"I'd like to see it," the townie said. "The school annual. When it comes out. I bet you win 'Prettiest Smile'."

It was one of the few times I had been drunk. I turned and looked at the townie.

"Your breath," he said. He touched my shoulder. "Your breath smells like gum."

The bartender checked with the other bartender. Heather was drinking from a red plastic cup someone had left on the bar. I had been drunk only a few times before and the townie was touching my shoulder.

"Do you know what it's like to be in this much pain?" the townie asked. He was shoving me now and putting his hands on my shoulders. "I'm so miserable, kid. I'm so miserable and I want you to put me out of my misery."

The bartender called for a bouncer. They were kicking us out because we were underage. I drained the last of the beer and turned to get Heather. Heather was coughing bits of mushrooms onto the bartop. She was sick. The townie was pulling me off of the barstool and telling me we had to leave.

"I want you to watch me shoot myself!" the townie shouted. "I want you girls to watch me shoot myself all over that lake."

The bouncers were kicking us out. The townie was pushing us toward the exit. The townie tried to hold my hand. Heather was already running down to the lake. The townie tried to kiss me. I ran after Heather in the dark.

Heather was sick. She was dunking her head into the lake. The beach was full of rocks. The water was green and still and the sky just above the mountains looked smoky in the moonlight. But it felt wrong to be in such a beautiful place with the townie and I wanted to go home. Heather was sick and I just wanted to go home.

HANC

The townie cursed the lake. He said he grew up in Detroit where there were assembly lines and tall buildings that touched the sky. He said machinery triumphed over nature. The destruction of all that we had loved as children seemed progressive to him and part of the advancement of civilization.

"It's the same thing with people," the townie said. "When you're a kid you can't see past your own backyard. That's why you think you have it so good. But you got to open your eyes. You got to see the big picture."

Heather had stopped being sick. She was gathering herself at the shallows.

"Hey," I said to the townie. "My friend's real fucked up right now. Just be cool and leave us alone."

"The scope of it," the townie said. "The scope of the real world is unthinkable."

Heather stepped out of the shallows and into the moonlight.

"We're going to California," she said to the townie. "You ever heard of it, you stupid shit? Hollywood. Fucking Orange County, USA."

"You have a disgusting mouth," the townie said.

Heather took another step toward the townie.

"Let's fight," Heather said. She put her fists in the air. "Let's fight, you stupid shit."

"Forget it, Heather," I said. "Let's get out of here."

Heather threw punches in the air. Her hair was plastered across her forehead in dark ropes.

"I was once an angel for Halloween," Heather said to the townie. "But you're the one who's dead inside. You're dead inside because nobody loves you and you don't love anyone."

Heather swung blindly and missed. The townie shoved her off.

"What's it like to be dead?" Heather said. She came at the townie again. "I'd like to watch you kill yourself so you can be dead on the outside too."

The townie knocked her down. There was blood under her nose.

"I'm contagious," the townie said. "I'm a contagious disease and I'm going to breathe my sickness on you."

I knelt down by Heather. She was crying now that she had seen her own blood.

"Get off her," the townie said.

"Just go, man. Give us a break," I said.

The townie grabbed my shoulder and pulled. "Let me see your face," he said. "Let me smell your breath."

He grabbed my shoulder again. I reached back and dug my nails into his hand. The townie raised his fist and punched me twice in the face. The sky was tilting and everything moved very slow. I heard Heather crying. There was a tooth in the back of my throat. I could barely see the townie coming toward Heather. She was so scared she hardly moved at all. She said my name. She said my name over and over again until she was made not to talk.

I saw her legs. They were thin and soft-looking. Even her socks were sad.

I saw her shoes. Sometimes her shoes were perfectly still. Sometimes her shoes showed hopeful signs of a struggle. Then her shoes were perfectly still again.

I saw her fingers. Her fingers were tiny and had rings on them. The tiny fingers spasmed and clawed at the soil as if something valuable was buried there.

I saw her knees. The knees were raised. There was a Band-aid on one of her knees.

For a moment I saw her stomach. She had an outie belly button. The outie had this silly little tip at the end.

There was mud underneath her chin. Her chin bucked. I could not see her eyes. I imagined her eyes not looking for God.

I saw her hair. Her hair was spread across the ground. She had always had the most beautiful hair and now it looked very dirty.

When she turned her head I saw her ear. Her ear was shaped like a question mark. I could only guess what her ear was hearing. I

BETWEEN   THE   RAIN   89

hoped it was Ziggy or Tom Petty. She had always wanted me to try Tom Petty and I never did.

The townie had left us to die on the lake. But Heather and I did not die. We refused to die the way he expected us to. We refused to die on the inside. Instead we caught the bus back home. The bus driver let us ride for free.

That night I gave Heather a bath. I brushed her hair and dressed her for bed.

"I'd never had sex before," Heather said.

"I know, baby," I said. I put the hairbrush in the drawer.

"My center's gone," she said. "The good part in me."

"You still have good things in you, Heather," I said.

"Liar," she said. She turned over on her side and cried herself to sleep.

Three months had passed. Heather was pregnant by the townie. She refused to tell her father or to find the townie. We would sit up very late at night and she would tell me of all her killed aspirations. She confided in me everything about herself that she considered ruined. She would stare out the window for long periods of time and I did not always know what she was thinking. I asked her what she wanted to do.

"I can't tell my father about this," she said. "And I don't want the others to know."

"There are options," I said.

"There is only one option," Heather said. "We'll go down to this magical place and kill it."

In my resistance Heather nurtured what was left of my innocence. She acted motherly. She said the awful things of the world ended with swift irreversible decisions. We would sit up very late at night and get stoned and listen to Bowie. We misinterpreted most of the Ziggy Stardust period. The world really was ending and there was no point in having children.

That night we dropped California Sunshine and split a six-pack of beer.

"This will give my future a little validity," Heather said on the bus ride down to the lake. "Once this is done I believe that previously unavailable facets of life will suddenly bloom before me."

Our brains were fried. Our brains were fixed on only one acceptable outcome. There was no rain at first. The wind that came down from the mountains whispered horrible thoughts and results. The moon gave little light through the pine trees. The wind ruffled the edges of the water and everything around us was quiet. The acid made me want to talk but Kermit the Frog hushed me. Miss Piggy played the coquette. The Muppets put on a delightful little opera. Fozzy paraded through the bushes. Placido Flamingo was singing in my ear.

"Pretend I'm Floyd Patterson," Heather said. "And you're Vasile Tita. You can try to knock me out but you can't fight destiny. You've got seventy seconds to live and I want to see you dance before you die."

We spent a long time fucking around at the lake.

For a while my mother was there.

"I died, Pam," my mother said. "I died a year ago in Nevada."

The wind was blowing hard down at the lake. The trees moved in the wind and the water whipped up into these little waves. The shallows filled with water quickly.

"Someone would've contacted us," I told my mother. "That's what they do," I said.

"Not when you just disappear," my mother said. "Not when you've been killed and buried in the desert."

"Shut *up*," I laughed. "You were not."

"They killed me because they knew no one would miss me," my mother said. "Who would miss you if you died, Pam? Would anyone? Who would miss you if you died?"

And then she crystallized and broke into translucent pieces that looked like hard candy.

"It's a hunt," Heather said. She opened another beer and drank

HANC

from the can. "We've got to force the animal out of the brush. We've got to flank it on all sides and when we shoot we must aim for the heart."

Nothing was working and we were roaming the woods without much direction and sometimes we screamed and cried at the sky. Heather tried punching herself in the stomach but she could not bring herself to do it hard enough. I was crying.

"Oh, just stop that," I said.

"Hit me, Pam," she said. "Come on. You owe me this much. Hit me as hard as you can."

This was Heather who wanted a horse for Christmas. This was Heather who dreamt of waves and surfer boys. She was crying too. I did not know what to do for her.

"Let's go home," I said. "Let's get cleaned up and go home."

The wind picked up again and sent shivers along the lake. I saw all these white horses running through the sky and I felt like I was in two places at once. There was happiness somewhere up there in the sky with the white horses. I saw Pegasus drinking from the spring. The sky was raining golden bridles. But there was sadness and horror down here on earth and I did not know of any other way of getting closer to the sky. There were a few more beers left and I shotgunned one until it was gone.

"The beer is good tonight," I said.

"I used to hate you," Heather screamed at me. She was wearing this little white dress with flowers on it. "I used to hate you when we first met." She lifted the little white dress above her stomach.

"Hit me for all your lies," she said. "Break one of my ribs for all your lies."

"We never hated each other," I said. I was still crying and the rain came down and I could not see the white horses anymore. There were too many clouds in the sky. "I don't want to do this, Heather. Don't make me do this."

"You owe me this," she said. She stepped forward in the rain and slapped me across the face.

"I promise I won't leave you, okay?" she said. "I promise I won't leave you like your mother did if you just do this one thing for me."

There was blood in my mouth and all I wanted to do was die. But Heather would not let me die and I hated her for it.

"Maybe you could have it and then—" I started to say.

"It's father is *death!*" Heather screamed. "Don't you see that?"

"I tried to help," I said. "I was drunk, he'd hit me and I—"

"You gave up on me," Heather said. "You forgot about me."

"I love you, Heather, don't you know how much I love you?"

"I don't love you and I never have and I want you to hurt me for it."

It was all too terrible and so I turned and slapped Heather to end it.

"Good," she said. She was crying and could not talk clearly. "Good."

The rain fell harder. I was watching myself from a safe place in the sky and pretended I was a different person. The real me was with the horses in the clouds. I punched Heather in the face and blood sprayed from her nose and she started to moan.

"It's a boy, Pam," Heather said. "Don't you think it's a boy?"

"God, just shut up," I said. I clasped my hands together and made a double fist.

"I'd name him Wyatt," Heather said. "After that movie we liked."

It did not take that long. There was a gush of fluid and tissue and blood. It was very dark. Heather sat down in the shallows. We sat there for hours and everything floated away. Eventually we caught the bus back home. I stayed with Heather for a while after that. It did not stop raining for five days.

During those five days I sat by the window and watched the rain as Heather slept. It was hard not to feel alone while I was watching the rain and Heather was asleep beside me in her bed. I did not always mind feeling alone but this time it was different. I felt like I was going to be alone forever. I was afraid that Heather was going to die because of what we had done. It was an awful feeling and I spent a lot of time crying quietly by the window and listening to the rain. I did not want my crying to wake up Heather and I tried to be very quiet. But it is hard to cry quietly when you are listening to the rain fall. Sometimes the sound of my own tears made me cry harder and I tried hard to see the beauty in the rain falling so it would not make me so sad.

It was impossible not to think about death. I was not afraid of how I would die or how much pain I would feel. I was only scared that I was going to die. It would not matter how or why it happened. Only that it did happen. I hoped that my life was going to change and that one morning the rain would just stop and I would not feel so alone anymore. When you are with friends death does not haunt you so easily. It is only when you are not alone that life seems perfect.

During those five days Heather would wake up in the middle of the night and call out for me. She always knew where to find me in the dark. I was always sitting in the chair by her window and watching the rain. She would call out to me and I would sit down on the edge of her bed and just put my hand on hers or run my fingers through her hair. Her blankets had pictures of horses on them. There were rabbits on her pillowcase. We did not talk very much because neither of us had very much to say. All the talking was finished now and I would sit there until she fell asleep again. It was always easy to watch Heather sleep. After a few days she did not feel sick anymore and she slept peacefully. I was not afraid she was going to die anymore.

I thought a lot about how my life was going to change. I imagined a time when it was not raining in Cherry Glenn. I thought someone might come walking up the main road in the sunshine and show me how to be happy. I knew that happiness was something that someone had to show me. I could not learn it on my own. It was like love or friendship or trust or any of the other things that make our lives meaningful.

When I got tired I would climb into bed beside Heather and sleep. The rain was falling outside and Heather was not feeling so sick anymore. It was then when I first started dreaming of California and all the wonderful things we would find there.

Chapter Fifteen

Heather was the first to scream. Roy was dead in the shallows and sand was spraying up from the bank. I dropped back into the circle of trees with my shirt around my neck. The shooting was coming from the top of the woods. The oil lamps exploded.

My friends tried to make it out of the water. One of the bullets hit Tony in the chest. He fell back into the lake and floated there on his back. Water rushed in where his chest used to be. There was the smell of gunpowder and all around us branches were cracking and shapes moved through the brush. I was not sure what was happening and everything was moving so fast. Danielle had reached the muddy shoots that ran into the lake. Her hair was wet against her back. Then a bullet hit her in the leg and she fell into the muddy shoots and rolled back down toward the lake. I was only a few feet from her in the trees. You could see bone through the skin of her leg as she tried to climb back up the muddy shoots.

"Danielle, don't move," I said.

When she turned to look at me she saw her leg. She started to scream.

"Danielle, shut up!" I shouted.

"What is this?" Danielle asked. "What's happening?"

There was another shot and her face was gone. Her body slipped into the lake and floated there. I started to cry. Georgia was crawling toward her clothes. Billy was walking toward her. He was putting on his shirt and looking very confused. There was a moment of peace. There were no shots coming from anywhere. Billy reached Georgia and took her hand. He looked like he was about to kiss her.

"It's a joke," he said. He reached down to take Georgia into his arms and that was when I saw that he had been shot in the back. "This is just a joke," Billy said again. He took Georgia into his arms and he died while she was holding him. Georgia sat there holding Billy up to her chest. I did not think she knew he was dead.

"Billy, do you love me?" Georgia asked. "Say you love me. You do, right? I know you do."

She was kissing him on the mouth. They were having their first kiss and I did not think Georgia knew that Billy was dead. Georgia broke away from Billy and looked into his eyes.

"Don't leave me like this, Billy," she said. "There's still so much I need to tell you."

I first saw the blood in her mouth. Then her neck opened up in the moonlight. Their bodies rolled and separated in the water.

I slipped my shirt back on. Heather was just under the surface of the water in the shallows. Her hair was in her eyes. "Heather, can you hear me?" I said. "Stay there. Stay right there."

I waited. There was movement in the woods. Something pumped in the darkness.

I ran for it. I skidded along the bank and fell into the lake. I found Heather at the shore. I swung my arms under hers and tried swimming with her away from the shots. Her body resisted and I froze in the water and listened.

The radio announcer spoke of a riot on the football field. The Jaguars had won the district championship. Someone was running through the woods and for a time the shooting had stopped.

I dragged Heather out of the water and over to her clothes. I dressed her quickly. I looked back at the lake.

"Can you walk?" I asked.

"It's come for us," she said. "Just let it happen, Pam."

"It's the townies," I said. "Something's happened."

"It doesn't really matter who or what it is," Heather said.

I pulled her up and held her against me. The woods were very dark now and still without all the people and the shooting. There were flashing lights coming from the Last Watch.

I ran for the main road. Heather was very weak and I used all my strength to hold her up.

There was another shot and bark sprayed into my face. I kept running.

There were many shots that sounded like firecrackers. I ducked and rolled and lost Heather in the brush.

"Get up," I said. "Let's go."

Trees were exploding all around us. Branches snapped in the dark.

Heather reached out for my hand and grabbed it.

"Run as fast as you can," I said.

We reached the main road and collapsed.

There were townies all around.

"Get some help!" I screamed.

The townies only looked at me. Their arms were limp at their sides and their faces were slack in the moonlight. Two or three of the townies were dead on the ground.

"Christ, what is wrong with you?" I said. "Help us!"

The townies only stared. Up the road I saw headlights.

A cop car. A fire engine maybe.

"Pam," someone said.

I looked down at Heather. She was so small. She looked like she had fallen asleep.

Blood swelled in a dime-shaped hole in her chest.

I plugged the dime-shaped hole with my thumb.

"Just let it happen," she said.

And then Heather started to die.

Chapter Sixteen

From *Time Is On Our Side*; (Heather Thomas's Senior List of Memories):

"First & 4ever, 2 Pam, my 1 tru friend . . . ILU! Blu won't always
B the color! & the rest of the 'drive-in Saturday' gang: HP, RB,
GC, TM, TC, B MAC . . . Where would I B w/out U? Lake prtys, 6
per. highs, making tapes, beers under The bed . . . 'We live 4 just
these 20 yrs, do we have 2 die 4 the 50 more' . . . C ya Cherry
Glenn, I'm CA dreamin! Seniors '77!!"

They showed parts of the game on television. They showed the riot
breaking out in the stands and the townies running onto the field once
the game was over.

A boy who was friends with Hank showed me a film of the game
after we graduated in June.

The score was Jaguars 28, Wildcats 3. We had the ball on our own 35 with one and a half minutes left in the game. No time-outs remaining.

The second string had been in for approximately four plays when Coach Knox did a strange thing.

He pulled his second string and returned his first string to the field. The Jaguars were not going to fall on the ball. The Jaguars hated the Wildcats and wanted another touchdown.

We came out of the huddle with one running back, one tight end to the left, and one slot to the right. There was a wideout to the right and a flanker to the left.

The slotback darted across the formation. Roy Boxley dropped back and hit the wideout on a ten-yard curl. The wideout spun and gained an extra seven yards before he was brought down by the free safety. The clock was still running.

The second play began on our 48. Roy dropped back. The tight end and the slotbacks drove straight down the field. The outside receivers went down ten yards. Roy looked left. Then he threw right before the receiver cut. Derek Hoffman hauled it in and put down two feet before even being touched.

There was a gain of twelve. The clock had stopped.

The Wildcats returned to the field with extra defensive backs. 58 seconds left.

The slotback went in motion away from the formation. The running back took a jab step left. He then took the ball from Roy and followed a crushing block from the guard. With every defender playing the pass, the running back went wild for 22 yards.

The clock kept running.

Roy Boxley took the next snap and kneeled on the ball. The Jaguars cheering section screamed victory. There was shoving in the stands. The Jaguars band began playing the school fight song.

With nine seconds left Roy Boxley took another snap to end the game. He began to kneel. He then popped up quick and threw the ball to Norman Bricknell on a fade route.

Bricknell waltzed into the end zone.

The Jaguars cheering section went schizo.

The townies took the field before the film spliced and went dead.

I remember the church.

There was rain leaking through the roof and some of the parents found buckets where they kept the cleaning supplies and placed them throughout the room.

I remember there was a little bit of sun that day. The sun passed by the windows of the church. I spent a long time looking at the sun as the priest talked. The sun kept passing by the window or maybe the rain clouds were passing over the sun. Sometimes the church was filled with white light. When the light hit my face I felt a little piece of me dying. My father stood next to me and held my hand. Sometimes he had to hold me up as I cried.

The floor of the church was wet. I remember the footprints of all the parents who were passing through the church to get to their seats. I remember noticing that the footprints were different sizes. The small children who passed through the church did not understand that some-one had just died. They were only there to make small footprints on the floor of the church and to wear their finest clothes and to remind us that we grow up too fast. Some of the parents brought little toys for their children to play with in the pews. I listened to the jingle of some of the toys and watched the water form on the floor of the church.

And I did not want to make the children understand. I only wanted to listen to the sound of their toys in the church with the white light coming through the windows above. There were hymn books scat-tered on the floor of the church and sometimes their little feet kicked one away. The hymn books made a shuffling sound on the parts of the floor where there was no water.

I remember the people sitting in front of me. Their cries of pain were just like mine. Perhaps a week ago they cried for joy or love or relief. But today they cried for pain and our cries were the same. Our cries were the same because death had come to Cherry Glenn to take our children away and no one could explain why.

Death had come to Cherry Glenn the way other things come. Letters and storms and men without families or useful dreams. We had only not come to accept death into our lives the way we had accepted the other things. We were not ready to accept it and so we cried for this intrusion. We cried because it seemed impossible that our children were dead.

I remember the church. The high ceilings through which rain fell and the buckets on the floor. The flowers that many of the parents had delivered and had placed near the altar. I remember the parents who got up to speak and the tears they wept. The white light was coming through the church windows. You could still hear the rain falling outside but afterward it was quite sunny and beautiful. The rain had died down as we left the church and drove to where they were to be buried.

I do not want to write about the burials or all the time I spent inside the police station. I do not want to write about Darren Cormac or how many townies ended up dead that night in the gun fight. Though these are true parts of the story I am not ready to write them because I am not yet willing to suffer the loss. When you write things down you lose them to the rest of the world and you can never have those things back for yourself again. When I am ready to lose that part of me I will write about the funerals and be done with writing about my friends completely.

There are some things that are necessary to keep inside you longer than others and you understand this because you are human. Perhaps this story ends with the memories you keep to yourself·and refuse to share with anyone else. We all have these memories and we should not be hated for keeping them silent. We are only not ready to forget them.

CHAPTER SEVENTEEN

The houses along the beach were bright in the sunlight and the motels just off the water were crowded with people. Beach shacks ran up the green hills and from the beach shacks I could hear the shouts of children playing. The sea smelled like fresh laundry and the little fishing boats down by the docks bounced on the short break near the sand.

The van had overheated. I was sitting on the embankment that rose above the beach. The rays of the white sun stung my eyes and the land in front of me seemed dusted with gold. The town was filled with surf shops and Mexican restaurants. The people wore fishing hats and sandals and the people were young and very tan. Surfers bucked on the last waves of the day and there were little boys in inner tubes at the shore. There were people fast asleep under umbrellas on the beach. I wondered if it was the burning sun that kept death away or if it was that the town was always filled with young people. Or perhaps the people here had fought against death or at the least chose not to think about it as much. Everything around me seemed very much alive and it was something I had not experienced before. I decided to walk down to the beach.

The sand was hot and soft. I walked quickly down to the shore and got my feet wet. The water was perfectly clear and there were shells along the shore. There were mountains covered in mist at the other end of the sea and I wondered how long it would take a person to swim there. Down the beach there was a boardwalk with taquerias and fudge shops and places where you could make your own taffy. Mexican women pushed white carts on the sand. I bought a lime popsicle and a drumstick with chocolate in the center. The Mexican women spoke Spanish and wiped the sweat from their foreheads with red bandanas.

On the walk back to the van I had to avoids shards of broken glass in the sand. There were a few overturned barbecue pits and broken beer bottles. California beaches were like this. There were traces of carelessness with all this beauty and you had to do your best to avoid it. I walked the path to the embankment. I opened the back of the van and turned down the blankets.

Heather was still waking up. I handed her the drumstick with the chocolate in the center.

"What kind did you get?" she asked.

"Lime," I said.

"Can we switch?" she asked.

We switched and ate our food while sitting on the back of the van in the sunlight. After we ate we walked down to the boardwalk and played a few games of Skee-Ball. Heather got two fifties in a row and by the end we had enough prize tickets for two parachute men and a jawbreaker. After Skee-Ball I took Heather down to the beach and we sat together in the sand for a long time.

The white sun had turned yellow. We watched the surfers until it was dusk. Heather played with the parachute men in the sand. We talked only a few times just to say how beautiful everything was. The tide was coming in and we knew it was time to get back on the road. We walked back up the beach to the van.

At the gas station Heather told me she had heard of a whale who lived at Sea World. She wanted to go to the park and have her picture taken while feeding fish to the whale.

"In certain dreams animals can act as healers," Heather said.

I asked the station attendant how far it was to San Diego. He drew me a small map on the back of an old gas receipt.

"You want my advice," the attendant said, "you got to spend more than one day at the zoo. They got all these little habitats you don't even know about unless you look. The elephants, you'll see them right off the bat because they're so big. But the birds and the baby turtles and the little things whose names you don't know from Adam. That's where you'll do most of your exploring. That's where the beautiful stuff is."

I pumped the gas and paid the attendant.

"Thanks," I said.

"Make sure to get your hand stamped," the attendant said. "That way you can leave the park and come back in the same day."

The attendant waved to us. I pulled out onto the highway and maintained the speed limit. The radio was on and the sun was setting into the water. Heather was singing along with the radio. It was "Mystified" by Todd Rundgren and we were driving right next to the ocean. I was smiling. I had not really smiled for a long time.